Maigret in Montmartre

Georges

Maigret in

Simenon

Montmartre

Translated from the French by Daphne Woodward

A Harvest/HBJ Book
A Helen and Kurt Wolff Book
Harcourt Brace Jovanovich, Publishers
San Diego   New York   London

Library of Congress Cataloging-in-Publication Data
Simenon, Georges, 1903–1989.
[Maigret au "Picratts". English]
Maigret in Montmartre/Georges Simenon; translated from the
French by Daphne Woodward.
p.   cm.
Translation of: Maigret au "Picratts".
"A Helen and Kurt Wolff book."
ISBN 0-15-655162-4 (pbk.)
I. Title.
PQ2637.I53M255313   1989
843'.912—dc20   89-38059

Printed in the United States of America
First Harvest/HBJ edition 1989

A B C D E F G H I J

Maigret in Montmartre

F o r Jussiaume, the policeman, who passed the same spots on his beat at practically the same time every night, comings and goings of this kind were so commonplace that his mind registered them automatically, rather in the way that people living near a railway station notice the trains pulling in and out.

Sleet was falling, and Jussiaume had stepped into a doorway at the corner of the Rue Fontaine and the Rue Pigalle, to shelter for a moment. The red sign of Picratt's was one of the few still alight round there, and its reflected glow looked like splashes of blood on the wet cobblestones.

It was a Monday, when business is always slack in Montmartre. Jussiaume could have listed the order in which most of the night-clubs had closed. Now he saw Picratt's neon sign go out in its turn; the proprietor, a short, fat man who had put on a beige raincoat over his evening clothes, came outside to wind down the shutters.

A figure—it looked like a small boy—slipped out of the door and glided off down the Rue Pigalle, towards the Rue Blanche, keeping close to the wall. Two men emerged next, one of them with a saxophone case under his arm; they turned in the direction of the Place Clichy.

Almost immediately afterwards another man came out, and set off down the Rue Notre-Dame de Lorette; the collar of his coat was turned up.

Jussiaume did not know the names of these people; in fact he scarcely knew their faces; but like hundreds of others, they had a meaning for him.

He knew that the next to come out would be a woman wearing a very short, light-coloured fur coat and perched on exaggeratedly high heels—walking very fast, as though she were scared at being out alone at four in the morning. She lived only a hundred yards away. She had to ring the bell, because the house door was shut at this hour.

Then came the last two—women, together, as usual. They walked, talking in undertones, to the street corner a few feet away from where Jussiaume was standing, and there they parted. The older and taller of the two lounged away up the Rue Pigalle. She would be going to the Rue Lepic, where he had sometimes seen her enter a house. The other woman hesitated, glanced at him as though about to say something; and then, instead of turning down the Rue Notre-Dame de Lorette, as she usually did, moved off towards the *tabac* at the corner of the Rue de Douai, which was still lit up.

She seemed to have been drinking. She wore no hat, and her fair hair shone when she passed beneath a lamp. She walked slowly, stopping now and then as though talking to herself.

'Coffee, Arlette?' asked the owner of the *tabac*, an old acquaintance.

'Laced,' she replied.

And a few seconds later the familiar smell of rum warmed up in coffee was wafted on the air. Two or three men were standing drinking at the bar, but she took no notice of them.

'She looked very tired,' the proprietor declared later.

That was probably why she had another coffee, laced with a double portion of rum—after which she fumbled rather clumsily to get money out of her bag, and paid.

'Good night.'

'Good night.'

Jussiaume, the policeman, saw her coming back down the street, walking even more hesitantly than on the way up. As she drew level, she caught sight of him through the darkness, turned to face him, and said: 'I want to make a statement at the police station.'

'That's easy,' he replied. 'You know where it is.'

It was almost opposite, behind Picratt's, as it were—in the Rue de La Rochefoucauld. From

3

where they were standing they could both see the blue lantern above the door, and the cycle patrol's bicycles propped against the wall.

At first he thought she wouldn't go. Then he saw her crossing the road, and she vanished into the building.

It was half past four when she walked into the ill-lit office, where Sergeant Simon was alone except for one young policeman. She said again:

'I want to make a statement.'

'Go ahead,' replied Simon good-naturedly. He had been twenty years in the district and was used to this kind of thing.

The girl was heavily made-up, and the various ingredients had run into each other a bit. She wore a black satin dress under her imitation mink coat. She swayed slightly as she stood clutching the bar which separated the policemen from the public part of the office.

'It's about a crime.'

'There's been a crime committed?'

There was a big electric clock on the wall, and she looked at it as though the position of the hands might be significant.

'I don't know whether it's *been* committed.'

'Then it isn't a crime,' said the sergeant, with a wink at his subordinate.

'But it probably will be committed. In fact it's certain to be.'

'Who told you?'

She seemed to be laboriously following some train of thought.

'The two men, just now.'

'What two men?'

'Clients. I work at Picratt's.'

'I knew I'd seen you somewhere. You do the nude act, don't you?'

The sergeant had never set foot inside Picratt's, but he went past the place every morning and every evening, and he had noticed an enlarged photograph of this girl displayed outside, with smaller photos of the other two.

'So some clients have been talking to you about a crime—just like that?'

'Not to me.'

'Who to, then?'

'They were discussing it together.'

'And you were listening?'

'Yes. I didn't hear it all. They were on the other side of a partition.'

Sergeant Simon understood this point, too. When he went past the place while the cleaners were at work, the door would be open, and he could see a dark room with red curtains and upholstery, a gleaming dance-floor, and all along the walls, tables separated by partitions.

'Go on. When was this?'

'Tonight. About two hours ago. Yes, it must have been two o'clock. I'd only been on once for my act.'

'What did the two visitors say?'

'The oldest said he was going to kill the Countess.'

'What Countess?'

'I don't know.'

'When?'

5

'Probably today.'

'Weren't they afraid you'd overhear them?'

'They didn't know I was there.'

'Were you alone?'

'No. With another client.'

'Someone you know?'

'Yes.'

'Who?'

'His first name's Albert: I don't know his surname.'

'Did he hear them too?'

'I don't think so.'

'Why shouldn't he have heard?'

'Because he was holding my hands and talking to me.'

'Making love?'

'Yes.'

'While you listened to what was being said on the other side of the partition? Can you remember the actual words?'

'Not exactly.'

'Are you drunk?'

'I've had a drop, but I know what I'm saying.'

'Do you drink like this every night?'

'Not so much.'

'Were you drinking with Albert?'

'We had just one bottle of champagne. I didn't want to let him in for a lot of expense.'

'He isn't rich, then?'

'He's only young.'

'In love with you?'

'Yes. Wants me to throw up the job.'

'So you were with him when the two chaps came in and sat down in the next box?'

'That's right.'

'You didn't get a look at them?'

'I saw them from behind, later on, as they were leaving.'

'Did they stay long?'

'About half an hour.'

'Did they drink champagne with the other girls?'

'No. I think they ordered brandy.'

'And they began at once to talk about the Countess?'

'Not at once. I wasn't paying attention, to begin with. The first thing I heard was something like this:

' "You see, she's still got most of her jewellery, but at the rate she's going it won't last long." '

'What was the voice like?'

'A man's voice. A middle-aged man. When they went out I saw one of them was short, stumpy and grey-haired. It must have been him.'

'Why?'

'Because the other was younger, and it wasn't a young man's voice.'

'How was he dressed?'

'I didn't notice. I think he had a dark suit—black, perhaps.'

'They'd left their overcoats in the cloakroom?'

'I suppose so.'

'So he said the Countess still had some of her

jewels, but at the rate she was going they wouldn't last long?'

'That's right.'

'What did he say about killing her?'

The girl was really very young, though she did her best to seem a lot older than her real age. Sometimes, for an instant, she looked like a little girl on the verge of panic. At such moments, she fixed her eyes on the clock, as though that helped her to think. She was swaying to and fro, almost imperceptibly. She must be very tired. The sergeant noticed a slight smell of perspiration from her armpits, mingling with the scent of cosmetics.

'What did he say about killing her?' he asked again.

'I can't remember. Don't rush me. I wasn't alone. I couldn't listen all the time.'

'Albert was cuddling you?'

'No, just holding my hands. The older man said something like: "I've decided to finish it tonight." '

'That doesn't mean he's going to kill her, though. It might mean he's going to steal her jewels. Or perhaps she owes him money and he's decided to have her up.'

'No,' said the girl stubbornly.

'How can you tell?'

'Because that's not it.'

'He definitely spoke of killing her?'

'I'm certain that's what he meant to do. I don't remember the exact words.'

8

'You couldn't possibly have misunderstood?'

'No.'

'And that was two hours ago?'

'A little more.'

'And knowing a man was going to commit a crime, you waited all this time to come and tell us about it?'

'I was upset. I couldn't leave Picratt's before it closed. Alfonsi's very strict about that.'

'Even if you'd explained why?'

'He'd only have told me to mind my own business, I expect.'

'Try to remember just what was said.'

'They didn't say much, and I couldn't hear it all. There was music going on. And then Tania came to do her act.'

For the last few minutes the sergeant had been making notes—but in an offhand way, as though not really convinced.

'Do you know any Countess?'

'I don't think so.'

'Is there one who comes to the joint?'

'Not many women come. I never heard it said that one of them was a Countess.'

'You didn't manage to get a proper look at the men?'

'I didn't dare. I was scared.'

'Scared of what?'

'That they'd guess I'd overheard them.'

'What names did they call each other by?'

'I didn't notice. I think one of them was called Oscar, but I'm not sure. I think I've had too

9

much to drink. My head aches. I'd like to go to bed now. If I'd known you weren't going to believe me, I wouldn't have come.'

'Go and sit down.'

'Mayn't I go home?'

'Not yet.'

He pointed to a bench that stood against the wall, below the black and white sheets of official announcements.

Then, at once, he called her back.

'What's your name?'

'Arlette.'

'I mean your real name. Got your identity card?'

She took the card out of her bag and handed it to him. He read aloud: 'Jeanne-Marie-Marcelle Leleu, aged 24, born at Moulins, dancer, 42 ter., Rue Notre-Dame de Lorette, Paris.'

'So your name isn't Arlette?'

'That's my stage name.'

'Ever been on the stage?'

'Not in a proper theatre.'

He shrugged his shoulders and gave her back her card, after copying out the particulars.

'Go and sit down.'

Then, murmuring to his subordinate to keep an eye on her, he went into the next room, where he could telephone without being overheard, and rang up the central emergency service.

'That you, Louis? This is Simon, at La Roche-foucauld Station. There hasn't been a Countess murdered tonight, by any chance?'

'Why a Countess?'

'I don't know. It's probably a cock-and-bull

story. The girl seems a bit cracked, and in any case she's as tight as they come. Makes out she heard two chaps planning to bump off a Countess—a Countess who has jewels.'

'News to me. Nothing's come in.'

'If anything of the kind turns up, let me know.'

They chatted on for a time about this and that. When Simon got back to the outer office, Arlette had fallen asleep, as though in a station waiting-room. The resemblance was so striking that he even glanced automatically down at the floor, looking for a suitcase beside her feet.

*

At seven o'clock, when Jacquart arrived to take over from Sergeant Simon, Arlette was still asleep, and Simon explained the situation to his colleague. He noticed she was waking up just as he left, but he preferred not to wait.

She stared in astonishment at the newcomer, who had a black moustache. Then she glanced uneasily at the clock and leapt to her feet.

'I've got to go!' she exclaimed.

'Just a minute, please,' said Jacquart.

'What do you want now?'

'Perhaps the nap has refreshed your memory?'

She looked sulky now, and her face was shiny, especially along the line of her plucked eyebrows.

'I don't know anything more. I've got to go home.'

'What did Oscar look like?'

'Oscar who?'

The policeman was glancing through the report Simon had made out while she was asleep.

'The one who meant to murder the Countess.'

'I never said his name was Oscar.'

'What was it, then?'

'I don't know. I don't remember what I said last night. I was tight.'

'So you made up the whole story?'

'I don't say that. I did hear two men talking on the other side of the partition, but I could only catch a few words here and there. Perhaps I got it wrong.'

'Well then, why did you come here?'

'I tell you, I was tight. When you're tight things seem different and you're apt to get excited about nothing.'

'No one said anything about the Countess?'

'Oh, yes. . . . I think so. . . .'

'And about her jewels?'

'There was something about jewels.'

'And about finishing with her?'

'That's what I thought at the time. I was already sozzled by then.'

'Who had you been drinking with?'

'With several clients.'

'And with this chap Albert?'

'Yes. I don't know him either. I only know people by sight.'

'Such as Oscar?'

'Why are you always dragging in that name?'

'Would you know him again?'

'I've only seen his back.'

'Backs are quite easy to recognize.'

'I'm not sure. Perhaps.'

Struck by a sudden thought, she asked a question in her turn:

'Has anyone been killed?'

When he did not answer, she became very agitated. No doubt she had a terrific hangover. Her blue eyes were pale and washed-out, and her lipstick had spread, making her mouth look disproportionately large.

'Can't I go home?'

'Not just yet.'

'I've not done anything wrong.'

By this time there were several policemen in the room, working or swapping stories. Jacquart rang up the emergency service, where there was still no news of the death of a Countess; and then, to be on the safe side, telephoned to police headquarters at the Quai des Orfèvres.

The telephone was answered by Lucas, who had just come on duty and was still half asleep.

'Send her over to me,' he replied on the spur of the moment.

After which he thought no more about it. Maigret arrived a few minutes later, and glanced through the night's reports before taking off his hat and coat.

It was still raining. Clammy weather. Most people were bad-tempered that morning.

Just after nine o'clock, a policeman from the IXth *arrondissement* appeared at the Quai des Orfèvres with Arlette. He was a new man who did not know the building very well, and he knocked on several wrong doors, Arlette following him all the time.

Finally he happened on the inspectors' room, where young Lapointe was sitting on the edge of a table, smoking a cigarette.

'Sergeant Lucas's office, please?'

He did not notice that Lapointe and Arlette were staring hard at each other, and on being told that Lucas was in the next room, he shut the door again.

'Sit down,' said Lucas to the girl.

Maigret, as usual, was making a quick round of the offices before the new report came in, and happened to be there at the moment, standing by the fireplace and filling his pipe.

Lucas explained to him: 'This girl says she heard two men plotting to murder a Countess.'

'I never said that,' she retorted, in a manner which had entirely altered—it was now assured, almost aggressive.

'You said you'd heard two men. . . .'

'I was tight.'

'And you made up the whole thing?'

'Yes.'

'Why?'

'I don't know. I'd got the blues. I didn't feel like going home and I just sort of drifted into the police station.'

Maigret threw her a fleeting, speculative glance and then went back to his papers.

'So there was no truth in all that Countess story?'

'No. . . .'

14

'None at all?'

'I may perhaps have heard something about a Countess. You know how you sometimes catch a stray word and it sticks in your mind.'

'Last night?'

'Very likely.'

'And you built up your whole story on that?'

'Do *you* always remember what you said when you'd been drinking?' Maigret smiled. Lucas looked annoyed.

'Do you realize that's a legal offence?'

'What is?'

'Making a false statement. You may find yourself in the dock on a charge of . . .'

'I don't care if I do. All I care about is getting home to bed.'

'Do you live alone?'

'You bet I do!'

Maigret smiled again.

'And you can't remember the client with whom you drank a bottle of champagne and who held your hands—the fellow called Albert?'

'I can hardly remember anything. How many more times have I got to tell you? Everyone at Picratt's knows I was plastered.'

'How long had you been that way?'

'If you must know, it began yesterday evening.'

'Who were you with?'

'I was by myself.'

'Where?'

'All over the place. In different bars. You've never lived alone, or you'd understand.'

15

That sounded funny, addressed to young Lucas, who always tried so hard to look dignified.

The rain seemed to have set in; it would go on all day—a cold, steady drizzle from a lowering sky; the lights would be burning in all the offices, and there would be wet patches on the floors.

Lucas had another job on hand, a burglary in a warehouse on the Quai de Javel, and was in a hurry to get there. He looked at Maigret and raised his eyebrows, as though asking:

'What am I to do with her?'

Just at that moment the telephone rang. It was to summon Maigret for the report, and he turned away with a shrug which meant:

'That's your affair.'

'Are you on the telephone?' the sergeant asked Arlette.

'The concierge is.'

'Do you live in a hotel?'

'No, I have a flat of my own.'

'Alone?'

'I've told you so already.'

'You're not afraid of running into Oscar, if I let you go?'

'I want to go home.'

They couldn't keep her indefinitely, simply because she had told some yam to her local police.

'Ring me up if anything else happens,' said Lucas as he rose to his feet. 'You won't be leaving Paris, I suppose?'

'No. Why?'

He opened the door for her and watched her as she walked away down the long, broad corridor and paused uncertainly at the top of the stairs. People turned to look at her as she went by. She obviously belonged to a different world, the world of night, and it gave one a kind of shock to see her in this harsh winter daylight.

In his office, Lucas was conscious of the atmosphere she had left behind her: the place smelt of woman, almost of bed. He rang up the emergency service again:

'No Countess?'

'Nothing to report.'

Then he opened the door of the inspectors' office.

'Lapointe,' he called, without looking in.

Another man's voice replied:

'He's just gone out.'

'Didn't he say where he was going?'

'He said he'd be back at once.'

'Tell him I want him. Not about Arlette or the Countess. I want him to come to Javel with me.'

Lapointe came back a quarter of an hour later. The two men put on their coats and hats and set out for the Châtelet Metro station.

When Maigret returned from the Chief's office, where the daily report had been delivered, he lit his pipe and sat down to look through a pile of records, vowing that he would not let himself be interrupted before lunch-time.

It must have been about half past nine when Arlette left the Quai des Orfèvres. It never occurred to anyone to inquire whether she was going home by bus or by Metro. She may have stopped in a bar for a cup of coffee and a *croissant*.

Her concierge did not see her come in, but that was natural, because the house—just off the Place St. Georges—was a big place, humming with activity.

It was nearly eleven o'clock when the concierge started to sweep the staircase of Building B, and noticed with surprise that Arlette's door was ajar.

LaPointe, at the Quai de Javel, seemed absent-minded and preoccupied. Lucas thought he looked off-colour and asked him if he felt all right.

'I think I've got a cold coming on,' replied Lapointe.

The two of them were still questioning the people who lived near the burgled warehouse, when the telephone rang in Maigret's office.

'This is the Chief Inspector, St. Georges district.'

It was from the station in the Rue de La Rochefoucauld where Arlette had gone about half past four that morning, and where she had fallen asleep on a bench.

'My secretary tells me that Jeanne Leleu, alias Arlette—the girl who said she'd overheard some talk about murdering a Countess—was brought round to you this morning.'

'I know more or less what you mean,' said Maigret, frowning. 'Is she dead?'

'Yes. She's just been found strangled, in her room.'

'In bed?'

'No.'

'Dressed?'

'Yes.'

'With her coat on?'

'No. She was wearing a black silk dress. At least, so my men have just told me. I've not been round there yet. Thought I'd better ring you first. It looks as though she'd been talking sense.'

'She was undoubtedly talking sense.'

'Still no news of any Countess?'

'Nothing so far. It may take time.'

'Will you see about informing the finger-print people, and so on?'

'I'll ring them up and then go straight to the house.'

'I think that's the best thing. Strange business, isn't it? The sergeant on night duty here didn't take her too seriously, because she was drunk. See you in a few minutes.'

'Right you are.'

Maigret decided to take Lucas with him, but found his office empty and remembered about the Javel affair. Lapointe wasn't there either. Janvier had come in that moment, and had not even had time to get out of his cold, wet raincoat.

'Come along with me!'

As usual, Maigret put a couple of pipes in his pocket.

2

JANVIER brought the little police car to a stop beside the pavement, and the two men, after craning their heads simultaneously to check the house number, looked at each other in surprise. There was no crowd outside, no one under the arched entrance or in the courtyard. A policeman had been sent from the station, as a matter of routine, to keep order; but he was merely strolling up and down at a little distance.

They soon discovered the reason for this unusual calm. Monsieur Beulant, the local inspector, came out of the concierge's quarters to greet them, bringing with him the concierge herself, a large, placid, intelligent-looking woman.

'This is Madame Boué,' he said. 'She's the wife of one of our sergeants. When she found the body, she locked the door with her pass-key and came down here to telephone me. No one else in the building knows anything about it yet.'

Madame Boué bowed slightly, as though acknowledging a compliment.

'So there's nobody up there?' asked Maigret.

'Inspector Lognon's gone up with the police doctor. I myself have been having a long talk with Madame Boué—we've been trying to think what Countess the girl could have been speaking of.'

'I can't think of any Countess around here,' put in Madame Boué.

It was obvious from her manner, her voice and her way of speaking, that she was determined to be the perfect witness.

'The girl was harmless enough, poor thing. I didn't see much of her, because she didn't get home till the small hours and was asleep most of the day.'

'Had she been living here long?'

'Two years. She had a two-room flat in Building B, at the far end of the courtyard.'

'Did she have a great many visitors?'

'Hardly any.'

'Any men?'

'If any came I never saw them. Except at the very beginning. When she moved in, and her furniture was being delivered, I once or twice saw an elderly man. I thought at first he might be her father—short and very broad-shouldered, he was. He never spoke to me. So far as I know, he's never been back since then. But a great many people come here, especially as Building A is full of offices, so one doesn't notice them all.'

'I shall probably be back in a few minutes for another word with you,' said Maigret.

The house was old and shabby. Two dark staircases led off under the archway, one on either side, with imitation marble plates announcing a ladies' hairdresser on the *entresol*, a masseuse on the first floor, an artificial flower workroom on the second, a solicitor, and even a fortune-teller. The cobbled paving of the courtyard was glistening with rain, and at the far side, straight ahead of them, Maigret and Janvier saw a door surmounted by a large B in black paint.

They went up three flights of stairs, leaving muddy footprints all the way, and only one door opened as they passed—to reveal a fat woman, her sparse locks twisted into curlers, who stared at them in astonishment, stepped back and locked herself in.

They were met by Inspector Lognon, of the St. Georges district. He was as glum as usual, and the eye he turned upon Maigret said plainly: 'This would have to happen!'

The inevitability attached, not to the strangling of a young woman, but to the fact that, a crime having been committed in the district and Lognon sent to investigate, Maigret had immediately arrived in person, to take matters out of his hands.

'I haven't disturbed anything,' he said in his

most official tone. 'The doctor's still in the bed-room.'

No rooms would have looked cheerful in weather like this. It was one of those gloomy days that make you wonder why you came into the world and why you take so much trouble to stay in it.

The first room was a kind of sitting-room—pleasantly furnished, spotlessly clean, and, contrary to what might have been expected, perfectly tidy. The first thing Maigret noticed was the floor—the parquet was as well polished as if it had been in a convent, and there was an agreeable smell of beeswax. He must remember to ask the concierge, on the way out, whether Arlette did her own housework.

Through the half-open door of the bedroom they could see Dr. Pasquier putting on his overcoat and arranging his instruments in their case. On the white goatskin rug at the foot of the bed (which had not been disturbed) lay a body in a black satin dress: all they could see was one very white arm and a mass of shining, copper-coloured hair.

The most pathetic impression always comes from some absurdly trivial detail, and when, this time, Maigret felt a slight lump in his throat, it was because, while one of the girl's feet was still wearing its high-heeled shoe, the other was unshod, the toes showing through a mud-spattered stocking in which a ladder started from the heel and ran up beyond the knee.

'Dead, of course,' said the doctor. 'The fellow who did it held on to her until he'd made sure of that.'

'Can you say when it happened?'

'Not more than an hour and a half ago. There's no sign of stiffness yet.'

Maigret noticed behind the door, near the bed, an open cupboard in which dresses were hanging—nearly all evening dresses, most of them black.

'Do you think he caught her from behind?'

'Probably; I found no trace of a struggle. I send my report to you, I suppose, Monsieur Maigret?'

'If you please.'

The bedroom was neat and bright, not at all suggestive of a night-club dancer's room. Here, again, everything was in order, except that Arlette's imitation mink coat was flung untidily on the bed, and her handbag lay on an armchair.

Maigret explained:

'She left the Quai des Orfèvres about half past nine. If she took a taxi she must have got here about ten o'clock. If she came by bus or Metro it would be a little later, of course. She must have been attacked at once.'

He went over to the cupboard and looked carefully at the floor inside.

'Someone was waiting for her, hiding in here. He must have grabbed her by the throat the moment she'd taken her coat off.'

It had happened such a short time ago: the police were not often called in so promptly to the scene of a crime.

'You don't need me any longer, I suppose?' inquired the doctor.

The local inspector asked, in his turn, whether he need wait till the photographers and other experts arrived, and was glad to get back to his office, which was only a few yards away. As for Lognon, he stood in a corner looking sulky, expecting to be told that he, too, was no longer needed.

'You haven't found anything?' Maigret asked him as he filled his pipe.

'I had a look in the drawers. See what's in the left-hand one in the chest of drawers over there.'

It was full of photographs, all of Arlette. Some of them were for publicity, including those which were displayed outside Picratt's. These showed her in a black silk dress—not the day dress she had on now, but a skin-tight evening dress.

'You belong to this district, Lognon; did you ever see her turn?'

'I never saw it myself, but I know what she had to do. As you can see from these photos at the top of the pile, her "dancing" consisted of wriggling about, more or less in time to the music, while she gradually took off her dress—the only thing she had on. By the end of her act she was stark naked.'

Lognon's long, bulbous nose twitched and almost seemed to be blushing.

'Seems that's what they do in America—striptease, they call it over there. Just as the last stitch dropped off her, the light would go out.'

He hesitated, and then went on:

25

'Have a look under her dress.'

Seeing that Maigret, surprised, was waiting for more, he added:

'The doctor who examined her called me and showed me. She's completely shaved. And even out of doors she had nothing on beneath the dress.'

Why did they all three feel embarrassed? By tacit agreement they avoided looking at the body, which still had something wanton in its appearance, as it lay outstretched on the goatskin rug. Maigret only glanced at the remaining photographs, which were smaller—probably taken with an ordinary camera—and showed the girl naked, in the most erotic poses.

'Try to find me an envelope,' he said.

At which Lognon, the damn' fool, gave a silent sneer, as though he suspected his superior of taking the things away to gloat over privately in his office.

Janvier, meanwhile, had begun an inch-by-inch inspection of the other room, and this called further attention to a kind of discrepancy between the place and the photographs—between Arlette's home and her work.

In a cupboard they found a little oil stove, two very clean saucepans, plates, cups and cutlery, which showed that she used to cook at least some of her own meals. In a meat safe that hung outside the window, above the courtyard, there were eggs, butter, celery and two lamb chops.

Another cupboard was full of brooms, dusters

and tins of polish. From all this, in fact, anyone would have imagined the place to belong to some elderly, respectable, even rather fussy house-wife.

They looked in vain for letters or private papers. There were a few magazines lying about, but no books, except a cookery book and a French-English dictionary. And no photos of parents, of other girls or of boy-friends, such as most young women display in their rooms.

There were a great many pairs of shoes, with exaggeratedly high heels—most of them almost new. Arlette must have had a passion for shoes, or else her feet were sensitive and she had difficulty in fitting them comfortably.

Her handbag contained a powder-compact, an identity card and an unmarked handkerchief. Maigret slipped the identity card into his pocket. Then, as though he felt ill at ease in the two small rooms, where the central heating was turned full on, he said to Janvier:

'You wait here for the experts. I'll probably be back before long, but they'll be arriving any minute now.'

No envelope had been found, so he pushed the photos into the pocket of his overcoat, smiled at Lognon, known to his colleagues as 'the churl'—and made for the stairs.

There would be a long, tedious business to be gone through in the house: all the tenants would have to be questioned, including the fat woman with her hair in curlers, who seemed to take an interest in passers-by and might have caught sight of the murderer on his way up or down.

Maigret stopped at the concierge's room and asked her if he might use the telephone, which stood beside the bed, with a photo of her husband, in uniform, hanging above it.

'Lucas isn't back yet, I suppose?' he inquired when he got through to the Quai des Orfèvres.

He dictated to another inspector the particulars entered on the identity card, and went on:

'Get into touch with Moulins. Try to find out whether she has any relations left there. There should be people who knew her, anyhow. If her parents are still alive, have them informed: I expect they'll come straight up to Paris.'

He was walking along the street towards the Rue Pigalle when he heard a car pull up. It was the photographers. The finger-print people and the rest would be arriving too, and he was anxious to be out of the way while some twenty people bustled about in the two small rooms where the body was still lying as it had fallen.

*

To the left of Picratt's was a baker's shop and to the right a wine merchant's. At night the place showed up clearly, of course, with its neon-lighted sign standing out against the dark fronts of the neighbouring houses. But in the daytime anyone might walk past without even noticing that it was a night-club.

The façade was narrow, just a door and a window; and in the chilly light of this wet morning the photographs in the show looked melancholy and rather suggestive.

It was past noon by now. To Maigret's surprise, the door was open. One electric lamp was burning inside, and a woman was sweeping the floor between the tables.

'Is the proprietor here?' inquired Maigret.

The woman paused in her work and looked at him calmly.

'Why do you want to know?' she asked.

'I'd like to have a word with him.'

'He's asleep. I'm his wife.'

She must be over fifty—nearly sixty, perhaps. She was stout, but still alert, with fine brown eyes in a plump face.

'I am Inspector Maigret, of the Judicial Police.'

Even at this she showed no uneasiness.

'Please sit down.'

It was dark inside, and the red walls and hangings looked almost black. Only the bottles behind the bar, just inside the open door, caught some gleams of daylight.

The room was long and narrow, with a low ceiling. There was a small platform for the musicians, on which stood a piano and an accordion in its case; and on either side of the dance-floor the walls were divided, by partitions about five feet high, into boxes where clients could sit in comparative privacy.

'Must I really wake Fred?' asked the woman. She was wearing bedroom slippers and an old dress with a grey apron over it, and she had not yet washed or done her hair.

'Are you here at night?'

'I look after the cloakrooms and do the cooking if clients want a meal,' she explained.

'Do you live in this house?'

'Yes, on the *entresol*. There's a staircase at the back, leading from the kitchen to our own rooms. But we have a house at Bougival where we go on closing days.'

She seemed quite unperturbed. Her curiosity must have been stirred by the arrival of such an important member of the police force. But she was used to seeing all kinds of people, and she waited patiently for an explanation.

'Have you had this place for long?'

'It'll be eleven years next month.'

'Do you get a lot of clients?'

'It varies.'

Maigret caught sight of a card on which was printed, in English:

> *Finish the night at Picratt's,*
> *The hottest spot in Paris.*

He had forgotten most of his English, but realized that 'hottest' in this sense must mean exciting—or, on second thoughts, something a bit stronger and more precise than that.

The woman was still gazing calmly at him.

'Won't you have something to drink?'

She obviously knew that he would refuse.

'What do you do with these cards?'

'Give them to the porters at the big hotels, who pass them on to visitors—especially Americans. And at night, late, when the foreigners are beginning to get bored with the larger night-spots and don't know where to go next, the Grasshopper strolls about outside and hands cards to them. And he drops them into cars and taxis. We do our real business after the other places close. You understand?'

He understood. Most people, by the time they got here, had been wandering round Montmartre for some time without finding what they wanted, and this was their last shot.

'I suppose most of your clients are half drunk when they come in here?'

'Yes, of course.'

'Did you have many people last night?'

'It was Monday. There's never a crowd on Mondays.'

'From where you stand, can you see what goes on in this part of the place?'

She pointed down the room: at the far end, to the left of the musicians' platform, was a door marked 'Toilet'. To the right was another door, with no inscription.

'I'm nearly always there. We aren't keen on serving meals, but sometimes people ask for onion soup, *foie gras* or cold lobster. And then I go off to the kitchen for a few minutes.'

'Otherwise you stay in this room?'

'Most of the time. I keep an eye on the women, and at the right moment I come along with a box of chocolates, or some flowers or one of those satin dolls. You know how it's done, I expect.'

She was not putting on any airs. By this time she had sat down, with a sigh of relief, and now she shook the slipper off one swollen, shapeless foot.

'What are you trying to get at? I don't want to hurry you, but it'll soon be time for me to go and wake Fred. He's a man and he needs more sleep than I do.'

'What time did you get to bed?'

'About five o'clock. Sometimes I don't get upstairs till seven.'

'And when did you get up?'

'An hour ago. As you see, I'd finished sweeping.'

'Did your husband go to bed at the same time as you?'

'He went upstairs five minutes before me.'

'Has he been out of doors this morning?'

'He hasn't been out of his bed.'

This insistence on her husband's doings was making her a little uneasy at last.

'It's not him you're after, is it?'

'Not specially. But I'm after two men who came here last night, about two o'clock, and sat in one of the boxes. Do you remember them?'

'Two men?'

She looked round at each table in turn, as though searching her memory.

'Do you remember where Arlette was before her turn came round for the second time?'

'Yes, she was with her young man. I even told her she was wasting her time.'

'Does he often come here?'

'He's been two or three times lately. Every now and then a man does stray in like that and fall in love with one of the girls. As I always tell them, it's all right for once, but they mustn't let it keep on happening. They were both here, in the third box as you look in from the street— No. 6. I could see them from where I stood. He was holding her hands all the time, and talking away to her with the soppy expression they all get when they're in that mood.'

'And who was in the next box?'

'I didn't see anyone.'

'Not at any time in the evening?'

'You can easily make sure. The tables haven't been wiped yet. If there was anybody at that one there'll be cigar or cigarette ends in the ashtray, and the marks left by glasses on the table itself.'

She sat still, leaving him to go and look.

'I don't see anything.'

'If it had been any other day I wouldn't be so positive; but Mondays are so slack, we sometimes think it isn't worth opening. I wouldn't mind betting we didn't have a dozen clients in all. My husband will be able to tell you exactly.'

'Do you know Oscar?' he asked point-blank.

She didn't jump, but he had the impression that she became a little reticent.

'Oscar who?'

'An elderly man—short, square-shouldered, grey-haired.'

'I can't think of anyone like that. The butcher's name is Oscar, but he's tall and dark, with a moustache. Perhaps my husband . . .'

'Go and fetch him, if you don't mind.'

Maigret sat still, in the dark red tunnel of a room with the light grey rectangle of the open door at its far end, like a cinema screen with the dim figures of some old news-reel flickering to and fro across it.

On the wall opposite him was a photograph of Arlette, in the inevitable black dress which clung to her body so tightly that she seemed more naked than in the indecent photos he had put in his pocket.

That morning in Lucas's office, he had paid scarcely any attention to her. She was just one of the little night-birds of which Paris held so many. All the same, he had noticed how young she was, and felt that there was something wrong somewhere. He could still hear her weary voice—the voice they all have at daybreak, after drinking and smoking too much. He remembered her anxious eyes; he remembered how he had glanced automatically at her breast; and above all he remembered the smell of human female that emanated from her—almost the smell of a warm bed.

He had seldom met a woman who gave such a strong impression of sensuality: and that was out of keeping with her worried, childish face and still more out of keeping with the rooms he had just left—with the polished floor, the broom-cupboard and the meat safe.

'Fred will be down in a minute.'

'Did you tell him what I wanted to know?'

'I asked him if he'd noticed two men. He doesn't remember them. In fact he feels sure there weren't two men at that table. It's No. 4. We always refer to the tables by their numbers. At No. 5 there was an American who drank almost a whole bottle of whisky, and at No. 11 there was a whole party, with women. Désiré, the waiter, will tell you about that, this evening.'

'Where does he live?'

'In the suburbs. I don't know where exactly. He goes home by train every morning from the Gare St. Lazare.'

'What other employees have you?'

'The Grasshopper, who opens car doors, runs errands, and now and then hands out cards. And the musicians and the girls.'

'How many girls?'

'Apart from Arlette there's Betty Bruce. She's the one in the left-hand photo. She does acrobatic dances. And Tania, who plays the piano when she's not dancing. That's all, at present. Other girls come in, of course, for a drink in the hope of picking up someone; but they don't belong to the place. We like to keep it small, Fred and me—we're not ambitious, and when we've saved enough money we shall retire and settle down to a quiet life at Bougival. Ah, here he comes. . . .'

A man of about fifty—short, sturdy, very well preserved, his hair still black except for a touch of grey at the temples—came out of the kitchen, pulling on a jacket over his collarless shirt. He must have snatched up the first clothes that came to hand, for he was wearing his evening trousers and had bedroom slippers on his bare feet.

He, too, was quite calm—even calmer than his wife. He must have known Maigret by name, but it was the first time he had actually set eyes on him, and he came forward slowly, so as to observe him at leisure.

'I'm Fred Alfonsi,' he announced, extending his hand. 'Didn't my wife ask you to have a drink?'

As though to confirm something of which he was already sure, he went to No. 4 table and rubbed the flat of his hand across it.

'You really won't have anything? Do you mind if Rose gets me a cup of coffee?'

At this, his wife went off to the kitchen and disappeared. The man sat down opposite Maigret, his elbows on the table, and waited.

'You're sure there were no clients at that table last night?'

'Now see here, Inspector. I know who you are, but you don't know me. Perhaps before coming here you made inquiries from your colleague in the *brigade mondaine*. His men drop in on me from time to time—it's their job and they've been doing it for years now. They'll tell you, if they haven't already done so, that there's never been any funny business at my place, and that I'm quite a harmless chap.'

Maigret was amused at the contrast between the man's words and his appearance, for he had the broken nose and cauliflower ears of an ex-boxer.

'So when I say there was nobody at that table, you can be sure it's true. This is a small place, there are only a few of us to run it, and I keep an eye on everything, the whole time. I could tell you exactly how many people came in last night. I've only got to look at the tickets on the cash desk; they're numbered according to the tables.'

'It was at No. 5, wasn't it, that Arlette sat with her young man?'

'No—at No. 6. The even numbers—2, 4, 6, 8, 10 and 12—are all on the right. The odd numbers are on the left.'

'Who was at the next table?'

'No. 8? Two couples came in at about four o'clock—Parisians who'd never been here before, who'd come because they didn't know where else to go, and who soon decided it wasn't their kind of place. They had just one bottle of champagne and then left. We closed almost directly afterwards.'

'And you never saw, either at that table or any other, two men by themselves, one of them elderly and, judging by the description, rather like you in appearance?'

Fred Alfonsi, who must have heard this sort of talk before, smiled and rejoined:

'If you'd spill the beans I might be able to help you. Don't you think this cat and mouse game has been going on long enough?'

'Arlette is dead.'

'What?'

The man gave a violent start. He got up agitatedly, and shouted down the room:

'Rose! . . . Rose?'

'Coming in a minute. . . .'

'Arlette's dead!'

'*What* did you say?'

She came rushing out at an amazing speed for one so fat.

'Arlette?' she echoed.

'She was strangled this morning, in her bedroom,' went on Maigret, watching them closely.

'Well, I'll be . . . Who was the bastard who . . .'

'That's what I'm trying to find out.'

Rose blew her nose and was obviously on the verge of tears. She was staring hard at the photograph on the wall.

'How did it happen?' asked Fred, going over to the bar.

Carefully selecting a bottle, he filled three glasses and came over to give the first one to his wife. It was old brandy, and he put one of the other glasses, without comment, on the table in front of Maigret, who finally took a sip of it.

'She overheard a conversation here, last night, between two men who were talking about a Countess.'

'What Countess?'

'I don't know. One of the men seems to have been called Oscar.'

There was no reaction to this.

'When she left here she went to the local police

38

station to report what she'd heard, and they took her to the Quai des Orfèvres.'

'And that's why she was bumped off?'

'Probably.'

'What about you, Rose—did you notice any two men together?'

She said she had not. Both she and he seemed genuinely amazed and distressed.

'I can assure you, Inspector, that if there had been two men here I should know and I'd tell you. We can speak quite straight to each other. You know how this kind of joint works. People don't come here to see first-class turns or dance to a good band. And it's no fancy drawing-room either. You've read our announcement. They go first of all to other places, looking for a thrill. If they pick up some girl there, then they don't get this far. But if they don't find what they want, they end up here more often than not, and by that time they've had about as much as is good for them.

'I'm in with most of the night taxi-drivers and I give them good tips. And the doormen at some of the big night-clubs whisper this address to clients when they show them out.

'We mostly get foreigners, who imagine they're going to see something sensational.

'The only sensational thing was Arlette undressing herself. For about a quarter of a second, when her dress slipped right down to her feet, they saw her absolutely naked. To avoid trouble, I asked her to shave herself—that's supposed to look less shocking.

'After that she'd nearly always be asked over to one of the tables.'

'Did she go to bed with clients?' asked Maigret deliberately.

'Not here, in any case. And not in working hours. I don't let them go out before we close. They keep the men here as long as possible by encouraging them to drink and I suppose they promise to meet them when they come out.'

'And do they?'

'What d'you think?'

'Did Arlette, too?'

'She must have, now and then.'

'With the young man who was here last night?'

'No, not with him, I'm sure. He was there from the purest motives, you might say. He came in one evening by chance, with a friend, and fell in love with Arlette at first sight. He came again several times, but never waited till we closed. He probably had to get up early and go to work.'

'Had she any other regulars?'

'Hardly any of our clients are regulars, you must surely have realized that. They're birds of passage. They're all alike, of course, but they're always different.'

'Hadn't she any men friends?'

'I know nothing about that,' replied Fred rather stiffly.

Maigret glanced at Rose and said, a little hesitantly:

'I suppose you yourself never . . .'

'Oh, go ahead—Rose isn't jealous and she got

over that a long time ago. Yes, if you must know, I did.'

'In her flat?'

'I never set foot in the place. Here, in the kitchen.'

'It's always that way with him,' observed Rose. 'You hardly notice he's gone, before he's back again. And then the woman comes in, shaking herself like a ruffled hen.'

She laughed at the thought.

'You don't know anything about the Countess?'

'What Countess?'

'Oh, never mind. Can you give me the Grass-hopper's address? What's his real name?'

'Thomas. . . . He hasn't any other. He was a foundling. I can't tell you where he sleeps, but you'll find him at the races this afternoon. That's the only thing he cares about. Some more brandy?'

'No thank you.'

'Do you suppose the journalists will be coming round?'

'Most likely. When they get wind of what's happened.'

It was difficult to make out whether Fred was delighted or annoyed at the publicity he was liable to receive.

'Anyhow, I'll do all I can to help you. I suppose I'd better open as usual this evening? If you like to drop in, you can question all the others.'

When Maigret got back to the Rue Notre-Dame de Lorette, the police car was no longer there, and an ambulance was just taking away the girl's body. A few idlers were hanging round the door, but not as many as he had expected.

Janvier was in the concierge's lodge, making a telephone call. He rang off just as Maigret came in, and said:

'The report from Moulins has come through already. The Leleu couple—father and mother —are still living there, with their son who's a bank clerk. As for Jeanne Leleu, their daughter, she's small, snub-nosed, dark-haired, left home three years ago and hasn't given a sign of life since. Her parents aren't in the least interested.'

'The description doesn't fit at a single point, does it?'

'No. She's two inches shorter than Arlette, and she isn't likely to have had her nose straightened.'

'No phone calls about the Countess?'

'Nothing at all. I've questioned all the tenants in Building B. There are a great many of them. The fat, fair-haired woman who watched us go upstairs is cloakroom attendant in a theatre. She makes out she isn't interested in what goes on in the house, but she did hear someone go past a few minutes before the girl got home.'

'So she heard the girl go up? How did she know who it was?'

'Says she recognized the footstep. In actual fact she spends her time peering through the crack of her door.'

'Did she see the man?'

'She says she didn't, but that he came upstairs slowly, as though he were very heavy or had a weak heart.'

'She didn't hear him go down again?'

'No.'

'She's quite sure it wasn't one of the tenants from higher up the house?'

'She knows the step of all the tenants. I saw Arlette's neighbour, too—a waitress: I had to wake her up, and she hadn't heard a thing.'

'Is that all?'

'Lucas phoned to say he was back in the office, waiting for instructions.'

'Finger-prints?'

'Only ours and Arlette's. You'll get the report sometime this evening.'

'You haven't got an Oscar among your tenants?' Maigret asked the concierge, on the off chance.

'No, Inspector. But once, a long time ago, I took a telephone message for Arlette. It was a man speaking, with a provincial accent, and he said, "Will you tell her Oscar is waiting for her at the usual place".'

'About how long ago was that?'

'A month or two after she came to live here. It struck me particularly, because it was the only message that ever came for her.'

'Did she get any letters?'

'One from Brussels, now and then.'

'A man's writing?'

'No, a woman's. And not an educated one.'

Half an hour later, Maigret and Janvier were on their way upstairs at the Quai des Orfèvres, after stopping for a pint at the Brasserie Dauphine.

Maigret was hardly inside his office when young Lapointe rushed in, red-eyed and agitated.

'I've got to speak to you at once, sir.'

Turning away from the cupboard where he had been hanging up his coat and hat, Maigret looked at the young man and saw that he was biting his lips and clenching his fists, to keep himself from bursting into tears.

3

HE spoke between clenched teeth, with his back to Maigret and his face almost pressed against the window-pane.

'When I saw her here this morning, I wondered why she'd been brought in. Sergeant Lucas told me the story while we were on our way to Javel. And now I get back to the office, only to hear that she's dead.'

Maigret, who had sat down, said slowly:

'I'd forgotten for the moment that your name was Albert.'

'After what she'd told him, Sergeant Lucas ought not to have let her go off by herself, without any protection at all.'

He spoke like a small, sulky boy, and Maigret smiled.

'Come over here and sit down,' he said.

Lapointe hesitated, as though he felt resentful

towards Maigret too. Then, reluctantly, he came and sat down on the chair opposite his chief's desk. He still hung his head, staring at the floor, while Maigret sat gravely puffing at his pipe. The two looked rather like a father and son in solemn colloquy.

'You've not been here very long yet, but you must have realized by now that if we had to give police protection to everyone who comes to us with an accusation, you'd often have no time for sleep or even to swallow a sandwich. Isn't that so?'

'Yes, sir. But . . .'

'But what?'

'She was different.'

'Why?'

'Well, you can see she wasn't just talking for the sake of talking.'

'Tell me about it, now you're feeling a bit calmer.'

'Tell you about what?'

'Everything.'

'How I got to know her?'

'Yes. Begin at the beginning.'

'I was with a chap from Meulan, an old school-friend who's not often been to Paris. First of all we went out with my sister, then we took her home and went up to Montmartre together, just the two of us. You know the sort of thing. We went into two or three joints and had a drink in each, and as we came out of the last of them, a kind of gnome pushed a card at us.'

'Why do you call him a kind of gnome?'

46

'Because he looks about fourteen years old, but his face is all wrinkled in fine lines—the face of a man who's past his youth. At a short distance you'd take him for a little street arab, and I suppose that's why they call him the Grasshopper. My friend had been disappointed with the places we'd tried so far, and I thought he might get more of a kick out of Picratt's; so we went there.'

'How long ago was this?'

He thought for a moment and seemed quite astonished and rather upset by what his memory told him; but he was forced to admit:

'Three weeks.'

'And that was how you met Arlette?'

'She came to sit at our table. My friend, who isn't used to that kind of thing, took her for a tart. We had a row when we got outside.'

'About her?'

'Yes. I'd realized at once that she was different from the others.'

Maigret let this pass without a smile; he was cleaning one of his pipes with the greatest care.

'And you went back there the following night?'

'Yes—to apologize for the way my friend had spoken to her.'

'What had he actually said?'

'He'd offered her money to sleep with him.'

'And she refused?'

'Of course. I got there early, to make sure of finding the place more or less empty, and she allowed me to stand her a drink.'

'A drink, or a bottle?'

'A bottle. The proprietor won't let them sit down at a table if they're only offered a drink. It has to be champagne.'

'I see.'

'I know what you're thinking. All the same, she came and told the police what she knew, and she's been strangled.'

'Did she say anything to you about being in danger?'

'Not in so many words. But I knew there were some mysteries in her life.'

'Such as?'

'It's difficult to explain, and no one will believe me, because I was in love with her.'

He spoke the last few words in a lower voice, raising his head and looking his chief straight in the face—ready to take offence at the slightest suggestion of irony.

'I wanted to get her to drop the life she was leading.'

'You wanted to marry her?'

Lapointe hesitated; he was visibly embarrassed.

'I hadn't thought about that. I don't suppose I'd have married her right away.'

'But you wanted her to stop showing herself naked in a cabaret?'

'I know it made her miserable.'

'Did she tell you so?'

'It wasn't as simple as that, sir. Of course I understand it looks different from your point of view: I know what sort of women one generally meets in places like that.

'But for one thing it was very difficult to tell what she was really thinking, because she used to drink. Usually, as you know, they don't drink. They pretend to, so as to encourage the clients, but all they really take is some syrup or other, served in a little glass so that it looks like a liqueur. Isn't that so?'

'Nearly always.'

'Arlette used to drink because she *had* to. Nearly every evening. So much so, that before she went on for her act, Mr. Fred, the proprietor, had to come round and make sure she could still stand up.'

Lapointe had become so much at home at Picratt's that he spoke of 'Mr. Fred', just as the employees no doubt did.

'You never stayed till closing time?'

'She wouldn't let me.'

'Why not?'

'Because I'd let out that I had to get up early and go to work.'

'Did you tell her you were in the police?'

The young man blushed again.

'No. I told her I lived with my sister, and it was she who told me to go home. I never gave her any money. She wouldn't have accepted it. She would never let me order more than one bottle of champagne, and she always chose the least expensive kind.'

'Do you think she was in love with you?'

'Last night I felt sure she was.'

'Why? What did you talk about?'

'The same as usual—about her and me.'

'Did she tell you who she was and what her parents did in the world?'

'She admitted she had a false identity card, and said it would be terrible if her real name were found out.'

'Was she well educated?'

'I don't know. She certainly wasn't made for that job. She never told me about her past life. She only referred to some man she said she'd never be able to shake off—adding that it was her own fault, that it was too late now, and that I must stop coming to see her because it only made her unhappy to no purpose. That's what makes me think she was beginning to love me. She was clutching my hands hard, all the time she was talking.'

'Was she already drunk?'

'Perhaps. She'd certainly been drinking, but she was quite clear-headed. She was like that nearly every time I saw her—all strung up, with an expression either of grief or of hectic gaiety in her eyes.'

'Did you ever go to bed with her?'

Lapointe glared almost with hatred at his chief.

'No!'

'Didn't you ever ask her?'

'No.'

'And she never suggested it?'

'Never.'

'Did she kid you into believing she was a virgin?'

'She'd been forced to submit to several men. She hated men.'

'Why?'

'Because of that.'

'Because of what?'

'Because of what they did to her. It had happened when she was almost a child—I don't know the details—and it left its mark on her. She was haunted by the memory of it. She was always talking about some man she was terrified of.'

'Oscar?'

'She didn't mention his name. I suppose you think she was fooling me and that I'm a simpleton. I don't care if you do. She's dead, and that at least proves she was right to be afraid.'

'Didn't you ever want to go to bed with her?'

'Once I did,' he admitted, 'the first evening, when I was with my friend. Did you ever see her alive? Yes, of course—but only for a few minutes, this morning, when she was worn out. If you'd seen her as she usually was, you'd understand. . . . No other woman . . .'

'No other woman . . . ?'

'It's too difficult to explain. All the men who went there were wild to have her. When she did her act . . .'

'Did she go to bed with Fred?'

'She'd had to submit to him, the same as to the others.'

Maigret was trying to discover how much Arlette had given away.

'Where?'

'In the kitchen. Rose knew. She didn't dare to make a fuss, because she's so afraid of losing her husband. Have you ever seen her?'

Maigret nodded.

'Did she tell you her age?'

'I suppose she must be over fifty.'

'She's nearly seventy. Fred's twenty years younger than she is. It seems she was one of the most beautiful women of her day, and was kept by some very wealthy man. She's really in love with her husband. So she daren't show any sign of jealousy, and she tries to fix things so that everything happens in her own house. She feels it's less dangerous that way—you understand?'

'I understand.'

'She was more scared about Arlette than about any of the others, and she'd hardly let her out of her sight. But it was Arlette who practically kept the place going. Without her, they won't get a soul. The other girls are just the commonplace type you find in every cabaret in Montmartre.'

'What happened last night?'

'Did she say anything about it?'

'She told Lucas you were with her, but she only mentioned your Christian name.'

'I stayed till half past two.'

'At what table?'

'Number six.'

He spoke like one who was at home in the place—almost as though he belonged there.

'Was there anybody in the next box?'

'Not in number four. A whole crowd came in to number eight—men and women, a very noisy lot.'

'So if there had been anyone in number four you wouldn't have noticed?'

'Oh yes, I should. I didn't want anyone to hear what I was saying, so I got up every now and then and looked over the partition.'

'You didn't see, at any table, a short, thick-set, middle-aged man with grey hair?'

'No.'

'And while you were talking to Arlette, she didn't seem as though she were listening to any other conversation?'

'I'm certain she wasn't. Why?'

'Would you like to go on working on the case, with me?'

The young man looked at Maigret, first in surprise and then with a sudden flush of gratitude.

'You'll really let me, although . . . '

'Now listen—this is important. When she left Picratt's at four o'clock this morning, Arlette went to the police station in the Rue de La Rochefoucauld. The sergeant who took down her statement says she was very strung up, and not too steady on her feet.

'She talked to him about two men who came in and sat down at number four table while she was at number six with you, and said she had overheard part of their conversation.'

'Why on earth did she say that?'

'That's what I want to find out. When we know that, we shall probably be a lot further on than we are at present. And that's not all. The men were talking about some Countess that one of them was planning to murder. Arlette said that

53

when they left she got a clear view of them from behind, and that one of them was middle-aged, shortish, broad-shouldered and grey-haired. And that during the conversation she caught the name "Oscar", which seemed to be addressed to this man.'

'But I'm pretty sure I should have heard. . . .'

'I've been along to see Fred and his wife. They say the same—that table number four wasn't occupied at all last night, and that nobody corresponding to that description came into Picratt's. So Arlette must have had some information and wouldn't or couldn't confess how she'd come across it. She was drunk—you said so yourself. She didn't think the police would bother to check where the clients had sat during the evening. You see what I mean?'

'Yes. And what made her mention a name?'

'Exactly. She wasn't asked for one. There was no need for her to do it. So she must have had some good reason. She must have been giving us a clue. And that isn't all. At the police station she seemed very sure of herself; but when she got here, after the effect of the champagne had worn off, she was much less talkative, and Lucas had the impression she'd have been glad to withdraw everything she'd said. And yet, as we know now, she hadn't made it all up.'

'I'm certain she hadn't.'

'She went home, and was strangled by someone who was waiting for her, hidden in her bedroom cupboard. Someone who must have known her very well, known his way about her flat, and probably had a key to it.'

'What about the Countess?'

'No news so far. Either she hasn't been killed, or no one has found the body yet—it might be that. Did she ever say anything to you about a Countess?'

'Never.'

Lapointe stared down at the desk for a moment and then asked, in an altered voice:

'Do you think she suffered much?'

'Not for long. The murderer was very strong, and she didn't even struggle.'

'Is she still in her room?'

'She's just been taken to the mortuary.'

'May I go and see her?'

'When you've had something to eat.'

'What shall I do after that?'

'Go to her flat in the Rue Notre-Dame de Lorette. Ask Janvier for the key. We've already been over the place, but you, who knew her, may find a meaning in some detail that escaped us.'

'Thank you,' said the young man eagerly; he was convinced that Maigret was giving him this task solely as a favour.

Maigret took care not to mention the photographs, whose corners were sticking out from under a file that lay on his desk.

Someone came to tell him that five or six journalists were waiting in the corridor, clamouring for news. He had them brought in, told them only part of the story, but gave each of them one of the photographs—those which showed Arlette in her black silk dress.

'And you might mention,' he added, 'that we should be glad if a certain Jeanne Leleu, who must be going by another name now, would come forward. We promise her there'll be no publicity, and we haven't the slightest wish to make trouble for her.'

*

He lunched late, at home, and had time to read through Fred Alfonsi's file when he got back to the office. Paris still looked ghostly in the fine, misty drizzle, and the people in the streets seemed as though they were moving through a kind of aquarium, and hurrying to get out.

The proprietor of Picratt's had a bulky police file, but there was hardly any significant information in it. When he was twenty years old he had done his military service in the penal *Bataillons d'Afrique*— for at that time he was being kept by a prostitute who lived in the Boulevard Sébastopol, and had already been arrested twice for assault and battery.

Then, after an interval of several years, he turned up in Marseilles, where he was recruiting girls for several brothels in the South of France. He was twenty-eight years old by that time. He was not yet a leading light in the underworld, but he was already too big a man to soil his hands in fights in the bars of the Vieux Port.

He had no prison sentences during that period, though there was one narrow escape over a girl of only seventeen whom he had prematurely 'placed', with forged identity papers, in Le Paradis, an establishment at Béziers.

Then came another gap. All that was known was that he had gone to Panama with a cargo of women, five or six of them, aboard an Italian boat, and had gained a certain notoriety over there.

At the age of forty he was back in Paris, living with Rosalie Dumont, alias La Rose, a woman well into middle-age, who had a beauty parlour in the Rue des Martyrs. He was a keen race-goer and boxing enthusiast, and was thought to take bets as a sideline.

After a time he had married Rose, and together they had opened Picratt's, which was originally no more than a small bar with its own group of regular customers.

*

Janvier had gone back after lunch to the Rue Notre-Dame de Lorette. He was not in Arlette's flat, as he was still questioning the neighbours —not only the other tenants in the building, but the nearby shopkeepers and everyone else who might have any information.

As for Lucas, he was left alone to clear up the Javel burglary, and was thoroughly disgruntled about it.

It was ten minutes to five, and darkness had fallen long ago, when the telephone rang in Maigret's office, and he heard what he had been expecting all day.

'This is the Emergency Centre.'

'Is it about the Countess?' he asked.

'It's *a* Countess, at any rate. I don't know if she's the one you're after. We've just had a call from the Rue Victor-Massé. A few minutes ago the concierge discovered that one of her tenants had been murdered, probably last night. . . . '

'A Countess?'

'Countess von Farnheim.'

'Shot?'

'No, strangled. That's all we know so far. The local police are on the spot.'

A few moments later, Maigret jumped into a taxi, which took an endless time to get through the centre of Paris. Going along the Rue Notre-Dame de Lorette, he caught sight of Janvier coming out of a greengrocer's shop, so he stopped the cab and called to him:

'Jump in. The Countess is dead!'

'A real Countess?'

'I don't know. It's quite near here. The whole business is happening in this district.'

For Picratt's, in the Rue Pigalle, was scarcely five hundred yards from Arlette's flat, and about the same distance from the Rue Victor-Massé.

On this new occasion the scene was different from that of the morning, for a score of inquisitive idlers were hanging round the door of the comfortable, respectable-looking house.

'Is the Chief Inspector there?'

'He wasn't at the station. It's Inspector Lognon who . . .'

Poor Lognon! He was so eager to distinguish

himself, and every time he started on a case he seemed fated to have it taken out of his hands by Maigret.

The concierge was not in her quarters. The walls of the staircase were painted to imitate marble, and there was a dark red stair-carpet held in place by brass rods. The atmosphere was rather stuffy, as though all the tenants were old people who never opened their windows; and the place was strangely silent—not one door so much as quivered while Maigret and Janvier were on their way up. On reaching the fourth floor, however, they heard sounds, and a door opened to reveal the long, lugubrious face of Lognon, who was talking to a very short, very fat woman with a tight bun of hair on the top of her head.

They went into the room, which was dimly lit by a standard lamp with a parchment shade. The atmosphere here was more oppressive than in the rest of the house. They suddenly felt, without quite knowing why, as if they were far removed from Paris, from the outside world, from the damp streets with their crowded pavements, the screeching taxis, the hurtling buses with their abruptly grinding brakes.

The place was so hot that Maigret took off his overcoat at once.

'Where is she?'

'In the bedroom.'

The first room was a kind of drawing-room, or had been—but in these surroundings the usual names didn't seem to fit. The whole place looked, somehow, as though it had been put ready for an auction sale, with all the furniture in unaccustomed places.

There were bottles lying round everywhere, and Maigret noticed that they had all contained red wine—the coarse red wine that navvies drink straight from the bottle, to wash down their lunch-time sausage as they sit by the roadside. There was sausage too—not on a plate, but on a piece of greasy paper, mixed up with scraps of chicken; and chicken bones were strewn on the carpet.

The carpet itself was threadbare and incredibly dirty, and the rest of the furniture was no better—there was a chair with a broken leg, a sofa with tufts of horsehair escaping from it, and the parchment shade on the lamp was singed brown with long use, and quite shapeless.

Next door, in the bedroom, on a bed which had no sheets and had not been made for several days, lay a half-naked body—exactly half-naked, for the upper part was more or less covered by a bodice, while from waist to feet the puffy, livid flesh was bare.

Maigret's first glance took in the little blue specks on the thighs and told him that he would find a syringe somewhere at hand. He found two—one with a broken needle—on what served as a bedside table.

The dead woman appeared to be at least sixty, but it was difficult to judge. No one had touched the body as yet. The doctor had not arrived. But she had obviously been dead for a long time.

The cover of the mattress on which she lay had a long slit in it, and some of the stuffing had been pulled out.

There were bottles in this room, too, and scraps of food; and, right in the middle of the floor, a chamber-pot with urine in it.

'Did she live by herself?' asked Maigret, turning to the concierge.

The woman nodded, with pursed lips.

'Did she have many visitors?'

'If she had, she'd probably have kept the place a bit cleaner, wouldn't she?' retorted the woman—adding, as though she felt the need to defend herself:

'I've not set foot in here for at least three years, until today.'

'Wouldn't she let you in?'

'I didn't want to come.'

'Had she no servant or charwoman?'

'Nobody. Only a woman friend, as crazy as herself, who used to look in now and then.'

'Do you know her?'

'Not by name, but I see her sometimes in the streets round here. She's not quite so far gone yet. That's to say she wasn't when I last saw her, which was some little time ago.'

'Did you know your tenant was a drug addict?'

'I knew she was half crazy.'

'Were you concierge here when she took the flat?'

'I'd have taken care she didn't. It's only three

years since we came to the house, my husband and I, and she's been here for at least eight. I've done my best to get rid of her.'

'Is she really a Countess?'

'So it seems. At any rate she was married to a Count; but before that she can't have been any great shakes.'

'Was she well off?'

'I suppose so, for it wasn't starvation she died of.'

'You didn't see anyone going up to her flat?'

'When?'

'Last night or this morning.'

'No. Her woman friend didn't come. Neither did the young man.'

'What young man?'

'A nice-mannered, sickly-looking boy with long hair, who used to visit her and called her "Aunt".'

'You don't know his name?'

'I never concerned myself with her affairs. The rest of the house is quiet enough. The first-floor tenants are nearly always away, and on the second floor is a retired General. You see the style of the place. This woman was so filthy that I used to hold my nose as I went past the door.'

'Did she never have a doctor in?'

'I should think she did! About twice a week. Whenever she was really drunk, on wine or whatever it was, she'd imagine she was dying and ring up her doctor. He knew her, and was never in a hurry to come.'

'A local man, was he?'

'Yes—Dr. Bloch, who lives three houses further down the street.'

'Was it he you rang up when you found the body?'

'No. That wasn't my business. I got on to the police at once. First the inspector came, and then you.'

'Would you try to get Dr. Bloch on the phone, Janvier? Ask him to come along as soon as he can.'

Janvier began a search for the telephone, which he finally discovered in another, smaller room, where it was on the floor, surrounded by old magazines and tattered books.

Maigret continued to question the concierge.

'Is it easy for anyone to get into the house without your seeing them?'

'Same as in any other house, what?' came the sharp retort. 'I do my job as well as any other concierge—better than most—and you won't find a speck of dust on the staircase.'

'Are those the only stairs?'

'There's a service flight, but hardly anybody uses it. And if they do, they still have to come past my door.'

'Are you there all the time?'

'Except when I'm out shopping: even a concierge has to eat.'

'What time do you do your shopping?'

'About half past eight in the morning, as soon as the postman has been round and I've taken up the letters.'

'Did the Countess get many letters?'

'Only circulars. From shops that must have seen her name in the directory and got excited because she had a title.'

'Do you know Monsieur Oscar?'

'Oscar who?'

'Any Oscar.'

'Well, there's my son.'

'How old is he?'

'Seventeen. He's apprenticed to a carpenter in the Boulevard Barbès.'

'Does he live here with you?'

'Of course.'

Janvier, having made his call, came in to report:

'The doctor's at home He has two more patients to see and then he'll come at once.'

Inspector Lognon was keeping ostentatiously aloof all this time—touching nothing and pretending not to listen to what the concierge was saying.

'Did the Countess ever get any letters with a bank address on them?'

'Never.'

'Did she go out much?'

'She sometimes stayed in for ten or twelve days at a stretch—in fact I used to wonder if she wasn't dead, for there wouldn't be a sound out of her. She must have been lying in a stupor on that filthy bed. Then she'd dress up, put on a hat and gloves, and one would almost have taken her for a lady, except that she always had a kind of wild look on her face.'

'Did she stay out long, at such times?'

'It varied. Sometimes for only a few minutes, sometimes for the whole day. She'd come back loaded with parcels. Wine was delivered to her by the case. It was always that cheap red stuff —she bought it from the grocer in the Rue Condorcet.'

'Did the delivery man come into the flat?'

'He used to leave the case outside the door. I had words with him because he wouldn't use the back stairs—said they were too dark and he didn't want to fall on his nose.'

'How did you come to hear she was dead?'

'I didn't hear she was dead.'

'But you opened her door?'

'I didn't have to take the trouble—and I wouldn't have taken it.'

'What do you mean?'

'This is the fourth floor. On the fifth there's an old gentleman, partly paralyzed, and I do his housework and take him up his meals. He used to be in the Inland Revenue. He's been living in the same flat for years and years, and he lost his wife six months ago. You may have read about it in the papers; she was run over by a bus one morning at ten o'clock, when she was crossing the Place Blanche on her way to the market in the Rue Lepic.'

'What time do you go up to do his housework?'

'About ten o'clock every morning. On my way down I sweep the stairs.'

'Did you sweep them this morning?'

'Why wouldn't I have?'

'You go up once before that, with the letters?'

'Not right up to the fifth floor—the old gentleman doesn't get many letters and he's in no hurry to read them. The third-floor people both go out to work and leave early, about half past eight, so they pick up their letters as they go past my lodge.'

'Even if you're not there?'

'Even if I'm out shopping—yes. I never lock the door. I do all my marketing in this street, and I keep an eye on the house while I'm about it. Do you mind if I open the window?'

Everyone was hot. They had all moved back into the first room—except Janvier, who was searching through drawers and cupboards as he had done in the morning at Arlette's flat.

'So you only bring the letters up as far as the second floor?'

'That's right.'

'And this morning about ten o'clock, you passed by this door on your way up to the fifth floor?'

'Yes, and I noticed it was a crack open. That surprised me a bit, but not much. On my way down I didn't think to look. I'd put everything ready for my old gentleman, and I didn't need to go up again till half past four—that's when I take him up his supper. On the way down I noticed this door was still a crack open, and without thinking, I called out—not loudly:

' *"Madame la contesse!"*

'Because that's what everybody called her. She

had a foreign name, difficult to pronounce. It was quicker to say "Countess".

'There was no answer.'

'Was there a light on in the flat?'

'Yes. I haven't touched anything. That lamp over there was burning.'

'And the one in the bedroom?'

'Must have been, mustn't it, seeing it's on now and I didn't lay a finger on the switch ? I don't know why, but I felt there was something wrong. I put my head through the door and called again. Then I went in, though I wasn't keen—being very sensitive to bad smells. I peeped into the bedroom and then I saw . . .

'So I ran down to call the police. There was no one else in the house, except the old gentleman, so I went and told the concierge next door, who's an old friend of mine; because I didn't fancy being alone. Some people asked us what was the matter; and there were several of us round the door when the inspector there turned up.'

'Thank you, Madame——?'

'Aubain.'

'Thank you, Madame Aubain. You may go back to your lodge now. I can hear someone coming upstairs, and I expect it's the doctor.'

It was not Dr. Bloch as yet, but the medical examiner—the same one who had examined Arlette's body that morning.

As he came through into the bedroom, after shaking hands with Maigret and nodding in a vaguely gracious manner to Lognon, he gave an involuntary exclamation:

'What—again!'

The Countess's bruised throat showed clearly how she had been killed. And the blue specks on her thighs showed equally clearly that she was hopelessly addicted to drugs. He sniffed one of the syringes and said with a shrug:

'Morphia, of course!'

'Did you know her?'

'Never set eyes on her before. But I know a good few of her sort, in this district. I say—looks as though theft had been the motive, doesn't it?' He pointed to the slit in the mattress, where the horsehair was hanging out.

'Was she well off?'

'We don't know yet,' replied Maigret.

Janvier, who for some minutes had been picking at the lock of a drawer with his penknife, announced at this point:

'This drawer's full of papers.'

Someone with a young, light step came quickly upstairs and into the room. It was Dr. Bloch.

Maigret noticed that the medical examiner greeted the newcomer with no more than a curt nod, pointedly refraining from extending his hand, as he normally would do to a colleague.

4

DR. BLOCH'S skin was too sallow, his eyes
too bright, his hair black and oily. He had apparently not paused on his way to listen to the
gossipers in the street or to speak to the concierge. Janvier on the telephone had not told him
the Countess had been murdered—only that she
was dead and that the inspector wanted to speak
to him.

He had rushed upstairs, four steps at a time,
and now stood looking uneasily about him. Possibly he had given himself an injection before
leaving his surgery. He did not seem surprised
at being snubbed by the other doctor, and made
no protest. His manner suggested that he was
expecting trouble.

Yet the moment he stepped into the bedroom,
he showed relief. The Countess had been strangled, so her death was nothing to do with him.

69

In less than half a minute he had recovered his self-assurance and was even inclined to be bad-tempered and insolent.

'Why did you send for me rather than for some other doctor?' he began, as though feeling his way.

'Because the concierge told us this woman was your patient.'

'I only saw her a few times.'

'What illness were you treating her for?'

Bloch turned towards the other doctor, as though to indicate that he must know perfectly well.

'You've surely realized that she was a drug addict? When she'd overdone it she'd have a fit of depression—it's frequent with such cases—work herself into a panic, and send for me. She was terrified of dying.'

'Have you known her long?'

'It's only three years since I took over this practice.'

He could hardly be more than thirty years old. Maigret would have been ready to bet that he was a bachelor and had become addicted to morphia as soon as he set up in practice—perhaps even before he qualified. He must have had his reasons for settling in Montmartre, and it was easy to guess what type of patients he attracted.

He wouldn't last long, that was obvious. His goose was cooked already.

'What do you know about her?'

'Her name and address, which are on my register. And the fact that she'd been taking drugs for fifteen years.'

'How old was she?'

'Forty-eight or forty-nine.'

Looking at the emaciated body on the bed, at the thin, colourless hair on the head, it was difficult to believe that she had been no older.

'Isn't it rather unusual for a morphia addict to drink to excess as well?'

'It happens sometimes.'

The doctor's hands were slightly shaky, as a drunkard's are apt to be in the morning, and one side of his mouth twitched every now and then.

'I suppose you tried to cure her?'

'At first, yes. It was a pretty hopeless case, I made no headway. She would let weeks go by without sending for me.'

'Didn't she ever send for you because she'd run out of the stuff and had to get hold of some at all costs?'

Bloch glanced at the other doctor. No use lying about it—the answer was written, as it were, on the body and all over the flat.

'There's no need, I imagine, for me to give you a lecture on the subject. An addict who has got beyond a certain point simply cannot, without serious danger, be cut off from the drug. I don't know where she obtained her supply. I never asked her. Twice, so far as I can remember, I arrived here to find her almost crazy because it hadn't turned up, and I gave her an injection.'

'Did she ever tell you anything about her past life—her family, her background?'

'All I know is that she really was married to a certain Count von Farnheim—I understand he was an Austrian and a great deal older than she. They lived together in a big house on the Riviera; she mentioned that once or twice.'

'One more question, doctor: did she pay you by cheque?'

'No—in cash.'

'And you know nothing about her friends, her relations, or her sources of supply?'

'Nothing whatever.'

Maigret let it go at that.

'Thank you,' he said, 'that is all.'

Once again he felt disinclined to wait until the technical people arrived, and still more reluctant to answer the questions of the journalists who would soon be thronging in: he wanted to escape from this stifling, depressing atmosphere.

He gave some instructions to Janvier and went off in a taxi to the Quai des Orfèvres, where he found a message asking him to ring up Dr. Paul, the official pathologist.

'I'm just writing my report, which will be with you tomorrow morning,' said the doctor—all unaware that he would have another post-mortem to carry out before his day's work was over. 'But I thought I'd better tell you right away about two points that may have a bearing on your inquiries. The first is that in all probability the girl wasn't as old as her record makes out. She's supposed to be twenty-four, but according to the medical evidence she can't be a day over twenty.'

'You're sure of that?'

'Practically certain. And the second point is that she'd had a child. That's all I can say. And the person who killed her must have been very strong.'

'Could it have been a woman?'

'I don't think so. If it was, she must have had the strength of a man.'

'Haven't you heard about the second crime yet? You'll be wanted any moment in the Rue Victor-Massé.'

Dr. Paul grumbled something about a dinner engagement, and the two men rang off.

The early editions of the evening papers had printed Arlette's photograph, and as usual several telephone calls had been received. Two or three people were waiting in the ante-room. An inspector was attending to them, and Maigret went home to dinner. His wife, having seen the newspapers, was not expecting him.

It was still raining. He was wet, and went to change his clothes.

'Are you going out again?'

'I shall probably be out for part of the night.'

'Have they found the Countess?'

(The papers had said nothing as yet about the murder in the Rue Victor-Massé.)

'Yes. Strangled.'

'Well, don't catch cold. According to the wireless, it's going to freeze and there'll probably be ice on the roads tomorrow morning.'

He took a small glass of brandy before leaving, and went on foot as far as the Place de la République, to get a breath of fresh air.

His first idea had been to let young Lapointe deal with Arlette's case; but on second thought he felt that would be cruel in the circumstances, and decided to leave it to Janvier.

Janvier would be hard at it now. Armed with a photo of Arlette, he would be making the round of all the cheap hotels and lodging-houses in Montmartre, with special attention to the small places that let rooms by the hour.

Fred, of Picratt's, had hinted that Arlette, like the other women, sometimes went off with a client at closing time. The concierge of her house had been positive that she never brought anyone home with her. But it was unlikely that she went far. And if she had a permanent lover, perhaps she met him at some hotel.

Maigret had told Janvier to take the opportunity of inquiring about a man called Oscar, about whom the police had no information and whose name the girl had only mentioned once. Why had she—apparently—regretted her mention of him and lapsed into silence afterwards?

Being short-handed, Maigret had left Inspector Lognon in the Rue Victor-Massé, where the photographers would have finished their work by now; probably the body had been removed while he was at dinner.

When he reached the Quai des Orfèvres, the lights were out in most of the offices. Young Lapointe was in the inspectors' room, going through the papers found in the Countess's drawer, which he had been told to examine.

'Found anything, my boy?'

'I haven't finished yet. All this stuff is in confusion and it's difficult to sort it out. Besides, I'm checking everything as I go along. I've made several phone calls already, and I'm expecting several others—including one from the flying squad at Nice.'

He held up a postcard photograph of a big, opulent-looking place overlooking the Baie des Anges. The house was built in the worst sham-oriental style, complete with minaret, and the name, The Oasis, was printed in one corner of the card.

'According to these papers, she was living here with her husband fifteen years ago.'

'She'd have been under thirty-five then.'

'Here's a photo of the two of them, taken at that time.'

It was an amateur snapshot, showing the couple standing at the front door of the villa; the woman had two huge borzois on a leash.

Count von Farnheim was a small, dried-up man with a little white beard; he was well-dressed and wore a monocle. The woman was buxom and good-looking—the type that men would turn to stare at.

'Do you know where the marriage took place?'

'At Capri, three years before this photo was taken.'

'How old was the Count?'

'Sixty-five at the time of the marriage. It only

lasted three years. He bought The Oasis as soon as they got back from Italy.'

The papers were a jumble of bills, yellow with age, much-stamped passports, cards of admittance to the casinos at Nice and Cannes, and even a bundle of letters. Lapointe had not had time to look at these; they were written in an angular, rather Germanic script, and signed 'Hans'.

'Do you know what her maiden name was?'

'Madeleine Lalande. She was born at La Roche-sur-Yon, Vendée, and at one time she was in the chorus at the Casino de Paris.'

Lapointe seemed to look upon his present job as almost a penance.

'Nothing's turned up, I suppose?' he inquired after a pause. He was obviously thinking of Arlette.

'Janvier's seeing to it. I shall be taking a hand too.'

'Are you going to Picratt's?'

Maigret nodded, and walked away to his office next door, where he found the inspector who was dealing with telephone calls and visitors who claimed to identify Arlette.

'Nothing reliable so far. One old woman seemed so sure of herself that I took her to the mortuary. Even when she was faced with the body she swore it was her daughter. But the chap on duty put me wise. She's cracked. She's been claiming to recognize every woman who's been brought in there for the last ten years or more.'

The weather forecast might have been right for once, because when Maigret left the office it was colder, as cold as winter, and he turned up the collar of his overcoat. He reached Montmartre too early: it was only just after eleven, and the night life had not begun—people were still packed together in theatres and cinemas, the neon lights of the cabarets were being turned on one by one, and the uniformed doormen were not yet at their posts.

Maigret went first of all to the *tabac* at the corner of the Rue de Douai, where he had been scores of times and was recognized. The proprietor had only just come in, for he too was a night bird. In the daytime his wife ran the bar, with a team of waiters, and he took over from her in the late evening, so they only met in passing.

'What will you have, Inspector?'

Maigret had already caught sight of a figure to which the proprietor, with a sidelong glance, now seemed to be directing his attention. It could only be the Grasshopper. His head scarcely topped the bar at which he was standing, drinking a *menthe à l'eau*. He, for his part, had recognized Maigret, but was pretending to be absorbed in his racing paper, on which he was making pencil notes.

He might easily have been taken for a jockey—he was just the right size. It was uncanny to discover, on looking closely, that with his childish body went a wrinkled, grey-skinned face with sharp, darting eyes which seemed to take in everything, like the eyes of some restless animal.

He was not in uniform, but wore a dark suit which gave him the appearance of a small boy in his first long trousers.

'Was it you who were here this morning, about four o'clock?' Maigret asked the proprietor, after ordering a glass of *calvados*.

'Yes, as usual. I saw her. I know what's happened—it was in the evening paper.'

These people would make no difficulties. A few musicians were there, taking a *café-crème* before going off to their work. And there were two or three shady characters whom Maigret knew and who put on innocent expressions.

'What was she like?'

'Same as she always was at that time of night.'

'Did she come every night?'

'No, only now and then. When she thought she hadn't had enough. She'd drink a glass or two of something strong and then go off to bed—she never stayed long.'

'Not even last night?'

'She seemed rather on edge, but she said nothing to me. I don't think she spoke to anyone, except to give her order.'

'Did there happen to be a middle-aged man in the bar, short and thickset, with grey hair?'

Maigret had deliberately refrained from mentioning Oscar to the journalists, so there had been nothing about him in the papers. But he had questioned Fred on the subject, and Fred might have repeated his questions to the Grass-hopper, who . . .

'I didn't see anyone like that,' replied the proprietor—a little too emphatically, perhaps.

'You don't happen to know a man called Oscar?'

'There must be any number of Oscars in the district, but I can't think of one who fits your description.'

Maigret edged along a couple of paces, to stand beside the Grasshopper.

'Anything to tell me?'

'Nothing in particular, Inspector.'

'Were you at the door of Picratt's all last night?'

'More or less. I went a little way up the Rue Pigalle once or twice, to hand out cards. And I came here once, to get some cigarettes for an American.'

'You don't know Oscar?'

'Never heard of him.'

The Grasshopper was not the type to be over-awed by the police, or by anyone else. His common accent and street arab manner were no doubt assumed, because they amused the clients.

'You don't know Arlette's lover, either?'

'Did she have one? First I've heard of it.'

'You never saw anyone waiting outside for her?'

'Sometimes. Clients.'

'Did she go with them?'

'Not always. Sometimes they were hard to shake off and she had to come here to get rid of them.'

The proprietor, who was quite frankly listening, confirmed this with a nod.

'Did you ever come across her in the daytime?'

'In the morning I'm asleep, and in the afternoon I'm at the races.'

'Had she any woman friends?'

'She got on all right with Betty and Tania, but they weren't close friends. I don't think she and Tania hit it off too well.'

'Did she ever ask you to get drugs for her?'

'What for?'

'For herself.'

'Not she. She was fond of a glass, and even of several, but I don't think she ever took drugs.'

'In fact you know nothing about her.'

'Except that she was the most beautiful girl I've ever seen.'

Maigret hesitated, sweeping the grotesque creature from head to foot with an involuntary glance.

'Ever have a date with her?'

'Why not? I've got off with plenty of others —clients, some of them, in the mink, not only local tarts.'

'That's perfectly true,' interrupted the proprietor. 'I don't know what gets 'em, but they swarm round him like flies. I've known some— and they weren't old or ugly either—who've come here well into the night and hung about waiting for him for an hour and more.'

The gnome's wide, rubbery mouth stretched in a complacent, sardonic grin.

'Maybe they've their reasons,' he said with a lewd gesture.

'So you went to bed with Arlette?'

'Shouldn't have said so if I hadn't.'

'Often?'

'Once, anyhow.'

'Was it her suggestion?'

'She saw I wanted to.'

'Where did it happen?'

'Not at Picratt's, of course. D'you know the Moderne, in the Rue Blanche?'

This was a house of call with which the police were well acquainted.

'Well, that was where.'

'Was she good?'

'She knew her stuff.'

'Did she enjoy it?'

The Grasshopper shrugged. 'Even when a woman doesn't enjoy it she pretends to,' he observed, 'and the less she's enjoying herself, the more she feels obliged to pile it on.'

'Was she drunk that night?'

'She was the same as usual.'

'And with the boss?'

'With Fred? Did he tell you about that?'

The gnome paused for thought, and gravely drained his glass.

'That's no business of mine,' he replied at last.

'Do you think the boss fell for her?'

'Everyone fell for her.'

'You too?'

'I've told you all I had to say. D'you want me

81

to set it to music?' inquired the Grasshopper mockingly. 'Are you going to Picratt's?' he added.

Maigret went, without waiting for the Grasshopper, who would soon be at his post. The red sign of the night-club was already alight. The photos of Arlette were still in the showcase. The door and window were curtained, and there was no sound of music.

He walked in, and found Fred, in a dinner-jacket, arranging bottles behind the bar.

'I thought you'd be round,' he said. 'Is it true that a Countess has been found strangled?'

It was not surprising that he should have heard, since the thing had happened in his district. Besides, the news might have come over the wireless by now.

Two musicians—one a very young man with shiny black hair and the other, about forty years old, who looked sad and unhealthy—were seated on the platform, tuning their instruments. A waiter was putting final touches to the room. There was no sign of Rose; she must be in the kitchen, or perhaps still upstairs.

The walls were painted red, the lighting was bright pink, and things and people looked rather unreal in the atmosphere thus created. Maigret felt as though he were in a photographer's darkroom. It took him a little time to get used to the place. People's eyes seemed darker and more gleaming, while the outline of their lips disappeared, the colour sucked out of them by the pink light.

'If you're staying on, give your coat and hat

to my wife. You'll find her at the far end,' said Fred. 'Rose!' he called.

She came out of the kitchen; she was wearing a black satin dress with a little embroidered apron over it. She took away Maigret's coat and hat.

'You don't want to sit down yet, do you?'

'Are the women here?'

'They'll be down any minute. They're changing. We have no dressing-rooms, so they use our bedroom and wash-place. You know, I've been thinking carefully about what you asked me this morning. Rose and I have talked it over. We both feel certain that it wasn't by listening to clients that Arlette got her information. Come here, Désiré.'

This was the waiter, who was bald except for a ring of hair that encircled his head, and closely resembled the waiter on the poster advertising a well-known brand of *apéritif*. He was no doubt aware of the resemblance and did his best to foster it he had even grown side-whiskers for the purpose.

'You can talk quite frankly to Inspector Maigret. Were there any clients at table four last night?'

'No, sir.'

'Did you see two men come in together and stay for some time—one of them short, middle-aged and' (with a glance at Maigret) 'rather like me?'

'No, sir.'

'Who did Arlette talk to?'

'She was quite a long time with her young

man. Then she had a few drinks with the Americans at their table. That's all. Towards closing time she and Betty sat down together and ordered brandy. It's entered to her account—you can see for yourself. She had two glasses.'

A dark-haired woman now emerged from the kitchen, looked with a professional eye round the empty room, where Maigret was the only stranger to be seen, went over to the platform, sat down at the piano and began talking in a low voice to the two musicians. They all three looked across at Maigret. Then she struck an introductory chord, the younger man blew a few notes on his saxophone, the other sat down to the percussion instruments, and a moment later a jazz tune burst upon the air.

'It's important for people to hear music as they go past the door,' explained Fred. 'It'll probably be at least half an hour before anyone comes in, but when they do they mustn't find the place silent, or the men and girls sitting round like wax dummies. What can I offer you? If you're going to take a table, I'd rather make it a bottle of champagne.'

'I'd prefer a glass of brandy.'

'I'll give you brandy in your glass and put the champagne bottle on the table. You see, as a general rule, especially at the beginning of the evening, we only serve champagne.'

He took evident pleasure in his work, as though it were his life's dream come true. Nothing escaped his attention. His wife was already seated on a chair at the far end of the room, behind the musicians, and she, too, seemed to be enjoying herself. They must have looked forward for a long time to setting up on their own, and it was still a kind of game for them.

'I know—I'll put you at number six, where Arlette and her boyfriend were sitting. If you want to talk to Tania, wait till they play a rumba. Then Jean-Jean takes his accordion and she can leave the piano. We used to have a pianist, but when we took her on and I discovered she could play, I thought we might as well cut down expenses by using her in the orchestra.

'There's Betty coming down. Shall I introduce her?'

Maigret had already taken his seat in the box, like an ordinary client, and Fred now brought over a sandy-haired young woman in a blue shot-silk dress with spangles.

'This is Inspector Maigret, who's investigating the murder of Arlette. You needn't be frightened. He's O.K.'

The girl might have been pretty if she had not been as tough and muscular as a man. She looked almost like a young man in woman's dress—so much so that it was embarrassing. Even her voice added to the impression—it was deep and rather hoarse.

'Do you want me to sit here?'

'I should be glad if you would. Will you have something to drink?'

'I'd rather not just yet. Désiré will put a glass in front of me. That's all that's needed.'

She seemed tired and worried. It was hard to

realize that she was there to attract men, and she did not appear to have much illusion on the point.

'Are you Belgian?' he asked, because of her accent.

'Yes—from Anderlecht, near Brussels. Before I came here I was with a team of acrobats. I began when I was only a kid—my father belonged to a circus.'

'What is your age?'

'Twenty-eight. I got too rusty for that line of work, so I took up dancing.'

'Are you married?'

'I was, to a juggler. He walked out on me.'

'Was it with you that Arlette left here last night?'

'Yes, as usual. Tania lives near the Gare St. Lazare, so she goes down the Rue Pigalle. She's always ready before us. I live practically next door, and Arlette and I used to walk together to the corner of the Rue Notre-Dame de Lorette.'

'She didn't go straight home?'

'No. That happened sometimes. She'd pretend to turn to the right and then, as soon as I was round the corner, I'd hear her walking on up the street, to get a drink at the *tabac* in the Rue de Douai.'

'Why didn't she do it openly?'

'People who drink don't usually like to be seen hurrying off for a last glass.'

'Did she drink a great deal?'

'She had two glasses of brandy with me before we left, and she'd already had a lot of champagne. And I'm pretty sure she'd been drinking even before she got here.'

'Was she unhappy?'

'If so, she never told me about it. I think she was just disgusted with herself.'

Betty was perhaps in the same state of mind, for she said this with a dreary expression, in a flat, indifferent voice.

'What do you know about her?'

Two clients, a man and a woman, had just come in, and Désiré was trying to steer them to a table. Seeing the place was empty, they looked at each other hesitantly, and finally the man said, with an air of embarrassment:

'We'll come back later.'

'They've come to the wrong address,' remarked Betty calmly. 'This isn't the place for them.'

She made an effort to smile.

'It'll be a good hour before we get going. Sometimes we begin our programme with only three people watching.'

'Why did Arlette take up this job?'

Betty gave him a long look, and then murmured: 'That's what I often asked her. I don't know. Perhaps she enjoyed it.'

She glanced at the photos on the wall.

'You know what she had to do in her act? They're not likely to find anyone who can carry it off so well. It looks easy, but we've all tried it and I can assure you it takes a bit of doing. Because if it's done just anyhow, it looks indecent at once. It really has to be done as though one were enjoying it.'

'Did Arlette do it like that?'

'I sometimes wondered whether she didn't do it because of that! I don't mean because she wanted the men—very likely she didn't. But she had to feel she was exciting them, keeping them on tenterhooks. When it was over and she went off into the kitchen—that's the "wings" of this place, we go through there on our way upstairs to change—she'd open the door a crack and peep out to see what effect she'd produced—just the way actors peep through the hole in the curtain.'

'She wasn't in love with anyone?'

There was quite a long silence before Betty replied: 'Perhaps she was. Yesterday morning I'd have said no. But last night, after her young man left, she seemed upset. She told me she thought she was a fool. I asked her why. She said that if she chose, things could be quite different.

' "What things?" I asked her.

' "Everything! I'm fed up."

' "Do you want to leave this place?"

'We were talking quietly, so Fred shouldn't hear us.

' "It's not only this place," she said.

' "I knew she'd been drinking, but I'm certain she meant it.

' "Has he offered to keep you?" I asked.

'She shrugged her shoulders, and muttered:

' "It's no use, you wouldn't understand."

'We nearly quarrelled, and I told her I wasn't

88

so dumb as she seemed to think—I'd been through that kind of thing too.'

At this moment the Grasshopper, with a triumphant expression, ushered in some worthwhile clients—three men and a woman. The men were obviously foreigners; they must be in Paris on business or for a conference, for they looked like important people. As for the woman, they had picked her up goodness knows where—probably on the terrace of a café—and she looked rather uncomfortable.

With a wink at Maigret, Fred settled them at number four table, and handed them an enormous wine-list on which every imaginable variety of champagne was set forth. Hardly a quarter of it could have actually been in the cellar, and Fred recommended a completely unknown brand which doubtless showed him a profit of about three hundred per cent.

'I must go and get ready for my act,' sighed Betty. 'Don't expect anything wonderful. It's good enough for that lot, anyhow—all they want is to look at legs!'

The orchestra had started a rumba, and Maigret beckoned to Tania, who had come down from the platform. Fred nodded to her to accept the invitation.

'You want to speak to me?'

In spite of her name she had no trace of a Russian accent, and Maigret soon discovered that she had been born in the Rue Mouffetard.

'Sit down and tell me what you know about Arlette.'

'We weren't particularly friendly.'

'Why not?'

'Because she put on airs and I didn't like it.'

The words came out with decision. This was a girl with a very good opinion of herself, and she was not in the least intimidated by Maigret.

'Did you quarrel?'

'We did even go that far.'

'Did you never speak to each other?'

'As seldom as possible. She was jealous.'

'Of what?'

'Of me. She couldn't admit that anyone else could be in the very least interesting. She thought she was the only person in the world. I don't like that sort of thing. She couldn't even dance—never had a lesson in her life. All she could do was take her clothes off, and if she hadn't shown them everything she had to show, her act would have had nothing to it at all.'

'You're a dancer?'

'I was taking ballet lessons before I was twelve.'

'And is that the kind of dancing you do here?'

'No. Here I do Russian folk dances.'

'Did Arlette have a lover?'

'Certainly she did; but she must have felt he was nothing to be proud of, so she never mentioned him. All I know is, he was old.'

'How do you know that?'

'We all undress together, upstairs. Several times I've seen bruises on her. She'd try to hide them with a coat of cream, but I have sharp eyes.'

'Did you ask her about them?'

'Once. She told me she'd fallen downstairs.

But she can't have fallen downstairs every week. And when I noticed the position of the bruises, I understood. Only old men have those nasty habits.'

'When did you first notice this?'

'At least six months ago, almost as soon as I began to work here.'

'And it went on?'

'I didn't look at her every night, but I often noticed bruises. Anything else you want to ask me? It's time I went back to the piano.'

As soon as she had taken her seat again, the lights went out, a spotlight was turned on the dance-floor, and Betty Bruce bounded into the middle of it. Behind him, Maigret could hear men's voices trying to speak French, and a woman's voice teaching them how to say *'Voulez-vous coucher avec moi?'* They were laughing and repeating, one after another, *'Vo-lez vo . . .'*

Fred came across without a word, his shirt-front glimmering through the darkness, and sat down opposite Maigret. Betty Bruce, keeping approximate time to the music, stretched one leg straight in the air and hopped about on the other foot, her tights clinging closely to her body and a strained smile on her face. Then she let herself fall to the floor, doing the splits.

5

WHEN his wife woke him with his morning coffee, Maigret's first thought was that he had not had enough sleep and that his head was aching. Then, opening his eyes wide, he wondered why his wife was looking so brisk, as though she had a delightful surprise for him.

'Look!' she said, as soon as his rather shaky hands had grasped the cup.

She drew back the curtain, and he saw that it was snowing outside.

He was pleased, of course; but there was a muddy taste in his mouth which indicated that he must have had more to drink than he had realized at the time. That was probably because Désiré, the waiter, had opened the bottle of champagne that was only supposed to be there for show, and he had poured himself some, without thinking, between two glasses of brandy.

'I don't know if it will settle, but anyhow it's more cheerful than the rain.'

Maigret didn't very much care whether it settled or not. He liked every kind of weather—especially the extreme kinds, which were reported in the papers next day—torrential rain, hurricanes, bitter cold or scorching heat. He liked snow, too, because it reminded him of his childhood; but he wondered how his wife could find it cheerful in Paris—especially that morning. The sky was even heavier than on the previous day, and against the white snow, the black, shiny roofs looked still blacker, the houses still more drab and dirty, and the curtains at most of the windows still dingier than usual.

It took him some time, while eating his breakfast and getting dressed, to sort out his memories of the night before. He had not had much sleep. He had stayed at Picratt's till it closed—that was at least half past four—and then he had felt he ought to imitate Arlette by calling at the *tabac* in the Rue de Douai for a final glass.

He would have been hard put to it to give a brief summary of what he had found out. For long periods he had sat alone in his box, puffing slowly at his pipe and gazing at the dance-floor or the clients, in that strange light which made everything look unreal.

As a matter of fact, he reflected, he could have left earlier: he had stayed on, partly out of indolence and partly because it amused him to watch the people, and the behaviour of Fred, Rose and the girls.

They made up a little world of their own, seeing practically nothing of the life that ordinary people lived. Désiré, the two musicians and the rest of them went to bed just as the alarm clocks were beginning to ring in most houses, and they slept through the greater part of the day. Arlette had led that life, not really waking up till she came into the reddish glow of Picratt's lamps, and seeing hardly anyone except the men who came here, who had had too much to drink and been brought in by the Grasshopper as they left other joints.

Maigret had watched Betty who, aware of his attention, responded by showing off her whole bag of tricks—with a sly wink at him every now and then.

Two clients had come in about three o'clock, when she had finished her act and gone upstairs to dress. They were already well lit up, and as the place was rather too quiet at the moment, Fred had vanished into the kitchen—evidently to call Betty back at once.

She had gone through her dance again—this time entirely for the benefit of the newcomers, waving her leg in the air right in front of their noses and ending up with a kiss on the bald pate of one of them. Before going away to change she sat on the other man's knee and took a sip of champagne from his glass.

Was that how Arlette went on? She was probably more subtle in her methods.

The men spoke a little French, but not much. Betty kept repeating, to them: *'Cinq minutes. . . .*

Cinq minutes. . . . Moi revenir . . .' and holding
up the fingers of one hand. She did come back
a few minutes later, wearing her spangled dress,
and called to Désiré of her own accord to bring
another bottle.

Tania, meanwhile, was busy with a solitary
client whose gloom deepened as he drank; he
held her by one bare knee and was no doubt
confiding his conjugal misfortunes to her at great
length.

The two Dutchmen's hands moved to and fro,
but never let go of Betty. They were laughing
loudly, their faces growing gradually redder, and
bottles were arriving at their table in rapid
succession. Once emptied, these bottles were
put under the table, and Maigret finally realized
that some of them had already been empty when
they were brought. That was the trick—as Fred's
glance admitted.

Maigret had got up once and gone to the
cloakroom. There was a lobby here, with brushes,
combs, and powder and rouge laid out on a
shelf, and Rose had followed him in.

'I've remembered something that may perhaps help you,' she said. 'It was seeing you come
in here that reminded me. It's usually here that
the girls get talking to me, while they're doing
themselves up. Arlette was no chatterbox, but
she did tell me a few things about herself, and
I guessed others.'

She offered him soap and a clean towel.

'She certainly didn't come from the same class
as the rest of us. She never talked about her

family to me, or to anyone else so far as I know, but she several times mentioned the convent where she had been to school.'

'Do you remember what she said?'

'If anyone spoke about some woman being harsh and unkind—especially about the sort of woman who puts on a good-natured air to cover her mean ways, Arlette would say softly:

' *"That's like Mother Eudice."*

'And one could tell she spoke from unhappy memories. I asked her who Mother Eudice was, and she said she was the person she hated most in all the world, and she had done her the most harm. She was the Mother Superior of the convent, and she'd taken a dislike to Arlette. I remember the girl once said:

' *"I'd have gone to the bad if it was only to spite her."* '

'She never told you what convent it was?'

'No, but it can't have been far from the sea, because she often talked in a way that showed she'd lived by the seaside as a child.'

Funnily enough, all the time she was talking, Rose was treating Maigret like a client, automatically brushing his coat-collar and shoulders.

'I believe she hated her mother, too. That was less definite, but it's the sort of thing a woman notices. One evening there were some real swells here, doing the rounds in style—including a Cabinet Minister's wife who really did look like a great lady. She seemed depressed and absentminded; took no interest in the show, drank very little, and hardly listened to what the others were saying.

'I knew all about her, and I said to Arlette—in here, as usual, while she was doing up her face:

' "It's brave of her to go about like this—she's been having all kinds of trouble lately."

'At which Arlette said, with a sneer:

' "I distrust people who've had troubles, especially women. They make that an excuse for trampling on other people."

'It's only a hunch, but I'd swear she was thinking of her mother. She never spoke of her father—if that subject came up, she'd turn her head away.

'That's all I can tell you. I always thought she was a girl from a good family, who'd kicked over the traces. They're the worst of all, that kind, and that would explain a lot that seems mysterious.'

'You mean her obsession about attracting men?'

'Yes. And the way she set about it. I'm no infant in arms myself. I did the same job at one time, and worse, as you probably know. But not the way she did. That's why there's nobody to take her place. The genuine ones, the professionals, never put so much energy into it. Look at them. Even when they let themselves go you can feel they're not really enjoying it.'

Fred came across to Maigret's table every now and then and sat down for a few words with him. On each of these occasions Désiré brought them glasses of brandy and water, but Maigret noticed that the liquid in Fred's glass was always the paler of the two. As he drank his own he thought of Arlette and Lapointe, sitting together in this same box on the previous evening.

Inspector Lognon would deal with the Countess, in whom Maigret felt little or no interest. He had known too many women of that kind—middle-aged, nearly always on their own, nearly always with a brilliant past life, who took to drugs and sank rapidly into utter degradation. There were probably a couple of hundred of them in Montmartre, and several dozen, slightly higher in the social scale, in comfortable flats in Passy and Auteuil.

It was Arlette who interested him, because he had not yet managed to place her, or to understand her completely.

'Hot stuff, was she?' he asked Fred at one moment.

Fred replied, with a shrug:

'Oh, I don't bother much about the girls, you know. It's quite true what my wife told you yesterday. I go to join them in the kitchen, or upstairs while they're changing. I don't ask them what they think about it, and the whole thing passes over very quickly.'

'You never met her outside this place?'

'In the street?'

'No. I mean, did you never make a date with her?'

He had the impression that Fred hesitated,

glancing towards the far end of the room, where his wife was sitting.

'No,' he said at last.

He was lying. That was the first thing Maigret discovered on arriving at the Quai des Orfèvres next morning (he was late and missed the report). The atmosphere in the inspectors' office was lively. Maigret began by telephoning to the Chief, to apologize and to say that he would come along as soon as he had heard what his men had to say.

When he rang, Janvier and young Lapointe came hurrying to his door in a neck-and-neck race.

'Janvier first,' he decided. 'I'll call you presently, Lapointe.'

Janvier looked as knocked-up as Maigret himself, and had obviously spent part of the night in the streets.

'I was rather expecting you to look in on me at Picratt's.'

'I meant to. But the further I went, the busier I got. In fact I haven't been to bed at all.'

'Found Oscar?'

Janvier took from his pocket a paper covered with notes.

'I don't know. I don't think so. I called at practically every small hotel between the Rue Châteaudun and the Montmartre boulevards, and showed the girl's photograph in all of them. Some of the proprietors pretended not to recognize her, or tried to dodge the question.'

'And the result?'

'She was known at at least ten of these hotels.'

'Did you try to find out whether she'd often been there with the same man?'

'That was the point I pushed hardest of all. Apparently she hadn't. It was usually about four or five o'clock in the morning when she turned up, and the men she brought were well loaded—probably clients from Picratt's.'

'Used she to stay long with them?'

'Never more than an hour or two.'

'Did you discover whether she took money from them?'

'When I asked that, the hotel-keepers looked at me as though I was cracked. She went twice to the Moderne with a greasy-haired young man who was carrying a saxophone case.'

'That'd be Jean-Jean, the musician from the night-club.'

'Perhaps. Last time was about a fortnight ago. You know the Hôtel du Berry, in the Rue Blanche? It's not far from Picratt's or from the Rue Notre-Dame de Lorette. She went there often. The proprietress was very talkative, because she's already had trouble with us about girls who were under age, and wants to put herself right. Arlette came there a few weeks ago with a short, broad-shouldered man whose hair was going grey at the temples.'

'Didn't the proprietress know him?'

'She thought she'd seen him about, but she didn't know who he was. She makes out he must be a Montmartre man. They stayed in their room until nine in the evening. That struck her particularly, because Arlette hardly ever used to come during the day or the evening, and usually went away again almost at once.'

'Get hold of a photo of Fred Alfonsi and show her that.'

Janvier, who had not met the proprietor of Picratt's, frowned at this name.

'If it was him, Arlette met him somewhere else as well. Wait a minute while I look up my list. At the Hôtel Lepic, in the Rue Lepic. It was a man I saw there—a fellow who's lost one leg and spends the night reading novels; says he can't sleep because his leg hurts him. He recognized her. She went there several times—usually, he told me, with a man he often sees in the Lepic market, but doesn't know by name. A small, thickset chap, who generally goes shopping late in the morning—without bothering to put on a collar, as though he'd just got up. Sounds rather the type, doesn't it?'

'Maybe. You'll have to make your round again, with a photo of Alfonsi. There's one in his file, but it's too old.'

'Will it do for me to ask him for one?'

'Ask him for his identity card, as though you were making a check-up, and get the photo copied upstairs.'

The office boy came in to say that a lady would like to speak to Maigret.

'Ask her to wait. I'll see her presently.'

Janvier went on: 'Marcoussis is going through the mail. He says there are a whole lot of letters

101

about Arlette's identity. And he's had about twenty phone calls already this morning. Everything's being checked, but I don't think there's anything reliable yet.'

'Did you ask everybody about Oscar?'

'Yes. None of 'em turned a hair. Sometimes they described some local Oscar, but it never sounded like our man.'

'Send Lapointe in.'

Lapointe arrived, looking worried. He knew his superiors must have been talking about Arlette, and wondered why he hadn't been called to join in their discussion, as usual. He gave an almost imploring look of inquiry at the inspector.

'Sit down, my boy. If there'd been anything fresh, I would have told you. We've not got much further since yesterday.'

'Did you spend the night up there, sir?'

'Yes, at the table you had the evening before. By the way, did she never tell you anything about her family?'

'All I know is that she ran away from home.'

'She didn't tell you why?'

'She told me she loathed humbug, and that she'd felt stifled all through her childhood.'

'Tell me frankly—did she treat you nicely?'

'What exactly do you mean by that?'

'Did she treat you like a friend—talk to you quite sincerely?'

'At times, I think. It's difficult to explain.'

'Did you begin making love to her right away?'

'I told her I loved her.'

'The first evening?'

'No. The first evening my friend was there, and I hardly opened my mouth. It was when I went back there by myself.'

'And what did she say?'

'She tried to make out I was only a kid, but I told her I was twenty-four—older than she was.

' "It isn't age that matters, my child," she retorted. "I'm ever so much older than you!"

'You see, she was very unhappy—in fact, desperate. I think that was why I fell in love with her. She'd laugh and joke, but she was bitter all the time. And sometimes . . .'

'Go on.'

'I know you think she was fooling me. . . . She'd try to make me stop loving her—she'd talk in a vulgar way on purpose, and use coarse words.

' "Why can't you just get into bed with me, like the rest of them? Leave you cold, do I? I could teach you a lot more than other women. I bet there's not one that has my experience and knows her stuff like I do. . . ."

'Oh, I've just remembered, she added: "I got my training in the right school." '

'Were you never tempted to try?'

'I wanted her. I could have screamed, sometimes. But I didn't want her like that. It would have spoilt everything, you understand?'

'I understand. And what did she say when you urged her to drop that kind of life?'

'She'd laugh, call me her little shrimp and begin to drink harder than ever, and I'm sure it was because she was desperate. You haven't found the man?'

'What man?'

'The one she called Oscar.'

'We haven't found anything at all so far. Now tell me what you did last night.'

Lapointe had brought in a thick file. It contained the papers found in the Countess's flat, which he had carefully sorted out; and he had written several pages of notes.

'I've managed to trace practically the whole story of the Countess,' he said. 'I had a telephone report from the Nice police first thing this morning.'

'Tell me about it.'

'To begin with, I know her real name—Madeleine Lalande.'

'I saw that yesterday on her marriage certificate.'

'Oh yes—I'm sorry. She was born at La Roche-sur-Yon, where her mother was a charwoman. Father unknown. She came to Paris to go into service, but within a few months she'd found a man to keep her. She changed lovers several times, doing a bit better with each one, and fifteen years ago she was one of the most beautiful women on the Riviera.'

'Was she already taking drugs?'

'I don't know, but there's nothing to suggest it. She was gambling, always in the casinos. Then she met Count von Farnheim, who came of an old Austrian family and was sixty-five years old at the time. Here are the letters he wrote her; I've arranged them according to date.'

'Have you read them all?'

'Yes. He was passionately in love with her.'

Lapointe blushed as though they were the kind of letters he himself might have written.

'They're very touching letters. He never forgot he was an old man, and almost infirm. At first they're full of respect. He calls her *Madame*, and later on *dear friend*, and finally *my dearest little girl;* he implores her to stay near him, never to leave him alone: he keeps on saying she's all he has in the world and he can't bear the thought of living his last years without her.'

'Did she become his mistress at once?'

'No. It took months. He fell ill, in a furnished house where he lived before buying The Oasis, and persuaded her to come there as a guest and spend a few hours with him every day. You can feel in every line that he's sincere, that he's clinging desperately to her, ready to do anything rather than lose her. He writes bitterly about the difference in their ages, and says he realizes he can't offer her a very pleasant life.

'*But it won't last long*, he writes in one letter. *I'm old and sick. In a few years you'll be free, little girl; you'll still be beautiful, and if you wish you'll be rich. . . .*

'He wrote to her every day—sometimes just short notes, like a schoolboy in love: "*I love you! I love you! I love you!*"

'And then, all of a sudden, he bursts into a

kind of Song of Songs, in an entirely different tone—speaking of her body, with a mixture of passion and a kind of reverence:

'I can hardly believe that your body has lain in my arms—that those breasts, those thighs. . . .'

Maigret gazed thoughtfully at Lapointe, without a smile.

'From that moment, he's haunted by the fear of losing her. And tortured by jealousy. He implores her to tell him everything, even if it gives him pain. He asks what she was doing the day before, what men she met. There's a lot about one of the musicians at the Casino, whom he thinks handsome and is terribly afraid of. He wants to know about her past life, too:

'I have to have you "all complete". . . .'

'And he ends by begging her to marry him.

'I've no letters from her. It looks as though she never wrote to him—just came to see him, or telephoned. In one of his last letters, writing again about his age, he says:

'I ought to have understood that that beautiful body of yours has cravings that I cannot satisfy. The thought is agony to me; whenever it comes into my mind, I feel as if I should die of torment. But I would rather share you than do without you altogether. I swear I will never blame you, or make scenes. You shall be as free as you are now, and your old husband will sit quietly in his corner, waiting for you to bring him a little happiness.'

Lapointe blew his nose.

'They went to Capri to get married, I don't know why. There was no marriage settlement, but they had a joint bank account. For a few months they travelled about, visiting Constantinople and Cairo; then they spent some weeks at a big hotel in the Champs-Elysées—I came across the hotel bills.'

'When did he die?'

'The police at Nice were able to give me all the particulars. It was barely three years after the marriage. They had been living at The Oasis for several months. They used to be seen driving in a big closed car with a chauffeur, going to the Casinos of Monte Carlo, Cannes and Juan-les-Pins. She was magnificently dressed and covered with jewels. They caused a sensation wherever they went, for she could hardly fail to attract attention and she always had her husband in tow—a small, shrivelled man with a little white beard and a monocle. People used to call him "the rat".

'She gambled heavily, flirted openly, and was thought to have several love-affairs.

'He would wait, like her shadow, till the early hours of the morning, with a resigned smile.'

'How did he die?'

'Nice is sending you the report by post, for there was an inquest. The Oasis stands on the Corniche, and has a terrace, fringed with palms, below which there's a sheer drop of about three hundred feet. Most of the places round there are like that.

'The Count's body was found one morning, lying at the foot of the precipice.'

'Had he been drinking?'

'He was on a diet. His doctor said he was apt to get fits of dizziness, because of some medicines he had to take.'

'Did he and his wife share a room?'

'No, they had separate suites. The previous evening they'd been to the Casino, as usual, getting back about three in the morning, which was unusually early for them. The Countess was tired. She explained frankly to the police that it was the bad time of the month for her, and she used to have a lot of pain. She went to bed at once. The Count, according to the chauffeur, went first of all to the library, which had a french window opening on to the terrace. He used to do that when he couldn't sleep—he was a bad sleeper. The theory was that he'd gone outside for air, and sat down on the stone balustrade of the terrace. It was his favourite place, because there's a view from there of the Baie des Anges, the lights of Nice and a long stretch of coast.

'There were no signs of violence on the body when it was found, and no trace of poison was discovered at the autopsy.'

'What happened to her after that?'

'She had to cope with a young nephew who turned up from Austria to dispute the will, and it was nearly two years before she won the case. She went on living at Nice, at The Oasis. She entertained a great deal—the house was very gay, and drinking went on till all hours. Very often the guests slept there, and the fun began again as soon as they woke up.

'The local police say she had several gigolos,

one after another, and they got away with a good deal of her money. I asked if that was when she began taking drugs, but there was no information about that. The police will try to find out, but it's a long time ago. The only report they've found so far is very scrappy, and they aren't sure they can lay their hands on the file.

'What they do know is that she drank and gambled. When she was well under way, she'd collect a bunch of people and take them home with her. So you can see there must be plenty of her crazy kind in that part of the world. She must have lost a lot of money at roulette; sometimes she'd stick obstinately to the same number for hours on end.

'Four years after her husband's death she sold The Oasis. That was in the middle of the slump, so she got very little for it. I think it's a sanatorium now, or a nursing-home. Anyway, it's no longer a private house.

'That's all that's known at Nice. After the house was sold the Countess disappeared, and she's never been seen again on the Riviera.'

'You'd better go and look in on the gambling-licence office,' advised Maigret. 'And the narcotics squad might have some news for you too.'

'Aren't I to deal with Arlette?'

'Not for the moment. I'd like you to ring through to Nice again, as well. They may be able to give you a list of the people who were living at The Oasis when the Count died. Don't forget the servants. I know it's fifteen years ago, but we may be able to trace some of them.'

It was still snowing, fairly hard; but the flakes were so light and feathery that they melted as soon as they touched a wall or the ground.

'Is that all, sir?'

'That's all for now. Leave the file with me.'

'You don't want me to write up my report?'

'Not till it's all finished. Off you go.'

Maigret got up: the heat of the office made him feel drowsy, and he still had a nasty taste in his mouth and a dull ache at the back of his head. He remembered there was a lady waiting for him in the ante-room, and decided to fetch her himself for the sake of walking a few yards. If there had been time he would have gone to the Brasserie Dauphine for a glass of beer to freshen him up.

There were several people in the glass-partitioned waiting-room, where the green of the armchairs looked harsher than usual, and an umbrella was standing in a corner, surrounded by a pool of melted snow. Looking round for his visitor, Maigret saw an elderly woman in black sitting bolt upright on a chair. She got up as he came in—she had probably seen his photo in the papers.

Lognon was there too, but made no move to rise; he just looked at the inspector and sighed. That was his way. He had a positive need to feel wronged, unlucky, a victim of circumstances. He had been working all night, trailing round the wet streets while hundreds of thousands of Parisians were asleep. The case was out of his hands now, since headquarters had taken it over.

But he had done his best, knowing that the credit would go to others; and he had made a discovery.

He had been sitting in the waiting-room for the last half-hour, together with a strange young man with long hair, a pale face and a thin nose, who stared straight ahead of him as though about to faint.

And naturally nobody paid any attention to him. They just left him to kick his heels. They didn't even ask who he'd brought with him, or what he'd found out. Maigret merely murmured: 'See you in a minute, Lognon!' as he showed the lady out.

Maigret opened the door of his office and stood back, saying: 'Please sit down.'

He soon realized he had made a mistake. Because of what Rose had said, and because of his visitor's respectable, rather prim appearance, her black clothes and stiff manner, he had assumed it was Arlette's mother, who had recognized her daughter's photograph in the papers.

Her first words did not correct this impression. 'I live at Lisieux,' she said, 'and I came up by the first train this morning.'

Lisieux was not far from the sea, and he seemed to remember that there was a convent there.

'I saw the paper yesterday evening and recognized the photograph at once.'

She put on a distressed expression, because she felt that would be expected; but she was not in the least upset. There was even a gleam of triumph in her little black eyes.

'Naturally, the girl has altered in the last four years, and that style of hairdressing makes her look different. But I have no doubt whatever that it is she. I would have gone to see my sister-in-law, but we have not spoken to each other for years now, and it is not for me to make the first advance. You understand?'

'I understand,' said Maigret gravely, with a little puff at his pipe.

'The name was different too, of course. But living the life she did, it was only natural she could have changed her name. However, I was puzzled to learn that she called herself Arlette and had an identity card in the name of Jeanne Leleu. The strange thing is that I used to know the Leleu family. . . .'

He waited patiently, watching the falling snow.

'Anyhow, I showed the photograph to three different people, reliable people who had known Anne-Marie well, and they all agreed that it was undoubtedly she—the daughter of my brother and sister-in-law.'

'Is your brother still alive?'

'He died when the child was only two. He was killed in a railway accident—you remember it, perhaps, the famous Rouen catastrophe. I'd warned him. . . .'

'Your sister-in-law lives at Lisieux?'

'Never left the place. But as I told you, we are quite out of touch. It would take too long to explain why. I am sure you will agree that there are some people with whom it is quite impossible to remain on friendly terms. Let us leave it at that!'

'Let us leave it at that!' he repeated.

Then he asked: 'What was your brother's name, by the way?'

'Trochain, Gaston Trochain. Ours is a large family, probably the largest in Lisieux, and one of the oldest. I don't know whether you are acquainted with the place. . . .'

'No, Madame. I have only passed through.'

'But you doubtless noticed the statue of General Trochain in the principal square. He was our great-grandfather. And the château with the slate-tiled roof that you see on your right as you go towards Caen, was our family property. It no longer belongs to us. It was bought by some *nouveaux riches* after the 1914 war. But my brother was comfortably off.'

'Would it be indiscreet to ask you what he did?'

'He was an Inspector in the Department of Civil Engineering. My sister-in-law was the daughter of an ironmonger who had made a little money, from whom she inherited nine or ten houses and a couple of farms. While my brother was alive she was accepted in society for his sake. But as soon as she was widowed, people began to realize that she had married above her, and now she is left practically alone in her big house.'

'Do you think she will have seen the newspaper?'

'Undoubtedly. The photograph was on the front page of the local paper that everyone sees.'

'Don't you find it strange that she has not got into touch with us?'

'Not in the least. She will certainly not do so. She is too proud. In fact I am convinced that if she were confronted with the body she would swear it was not her daughter. I know she had heard nothing from the girl for the last four years. Nobody had, at Lisieux. And she's not upset about her daughter—only about what people are thinking.'

'Do you know why the girl left home?'

'I should say nobody could stay under the same roof as that woman. But there was another reason. I don't know where the child inherited her character from; it was not from my brother, everyone will tell you that. But when she was fifteen, she was expelled from her convent-school. And after that, if I happened to go out in the evening, I never dared look at dark doorways, for fear of seeing her there with a man. Even married men, there were. My sister-in-law thought fit to lock her up, which has never been a wise method, and it only made her worse. People say she climbed out of the window once without her shoes, and was seen like that in the street.'

'Is there any distinguishing mark by which you would be sure of recognizing her?'

'Yes, Inspector.'

'What is it?'

'I have not been blessed with children myself. My husband was never very strong, and he has been an invalid for years now. When my niece was a little girl, her mother and I were still on friendly terms. As the child's aunt I often took care of her, and I remember she had a birthmark under her left heel—a small port wine mark that never faded out.'

Maigret picked up the telephone and asked for the police mortuary.

'Hello? This is the Judicial Police. Will you please look at the left foot of the young woman who was brought in yesterday? Yes. . . . I'll hold on. Tell me if you find any distinguishing point. . . .'

The woman waited with the complete self-assurance of one to whom misgivings were unknown—sitting very straight on her chair, her hands folded over the silver clasp of her handbag. One could imagine her sitting like that in church, listening to the sermon, with that same hard, secretive face.

'Hello? Yes. . . . That's all. . . . Thank you. Someone will be coming along to identify the body. . . .'

He turned to the lady from Lisieux.

'You're not afraid to go, I take it?'

'It is my duty,' she replied.

He had not the heart to keep poor Lognon waiting any longer: besides, he felt no wish to escort his visitor to the morgue. He went over and looked into the next-door office.

'Are you free, Lucas?'

'I've just finished my report on the Javel business.'

'Would you take this lady round to the mortuary?'

She was taller than Sergeant Lucas, and very stiff, and as she marched ahead of him down the corridor, she looked rather as though she were leading him on a string.

6

LOGNON came in, driving his prisoner in front
of him. Maigret noticed that the young man's
hair was so long that it made a kind of pad at
the back of his neck, and that he was carrying
a heavy brown canvas hold-all, clumsily mended
with string, its weight pulling him to one side
as he walked.

Opening the door that led to the inspectors'
office, the inspector signed to the young man to
go in there.

'See what's inside that,' he said to his waiting
subordinates, pointing to the hold-all.

About to close the door, he had a second
thought.

'Make him let his trousers down, to see if he's
got needlemarks.'

Alone with the gloomy Lognon, he turned
and looked at him benevolently. He was not

117

disturbed by the man's bad temper, and knew his wife did not lead him a very pleasant life. Some of the other men had tried to be friendly with Lognon. But he was too much for them. The mere sight of his glum face, with its perpetual air of foreseeing disaster, was enough to provoke a shrug or a grin.

Maigret rather suspected that he had developed a taste for bad luck and ill-temper and adopted them as his pet vices—gloating over them just as some old men gloat over their chronic bronchitis and the sympathy it earns for them.

'Well, old chap?'

'Well, here I am.'

That meant that Lognon was ready to answer questions, since he was a mere underling, but that he thought it outrageous to have to present a report—he, who would have led the investigation if it hadn't been for the Judicial Police— he, who knew his district inside out and had not allowed himself a moment's rest since the previous day.

His pursed lips said more clearly than words: 'I know what will happen. It's always like this. You'll pick my brains, and tomorrow or next day the papers will announce that Inspector Maigret has cleared up the crime. With the usual talk about his unerring instinct and his methods.'

Lognon, in fact, didn't believe in all that, and this probably accounted for his attitude. If Maigret was an inspector, and the other fellows here were in the Special Branch instead of kicking their heels in a district police station, it was only because they'd been lucky, or pulled strings, or knew how to make anything of themselves.

In his opinion, he was as good as the best of them.

'Where did you pick up that lad?'

'At the Gare du Nord.'

'When?'

'This morning, at half past six. Before it was light.'

'Do you know his name?'

'I've known it for ages. This is the eighth time I've arrested him. He's best known by his first name, Philippe. His full name is Philippe Mortemart, and his father is a professor at Nancy University.'

It was unusual for Lognon to provide so much information in one breath. His shoes were muddy, and as they were old they must have let the water in; his trousers were damp up to the knees, and his eyes were red-rimmed and weary.

'You realized at once who it was when the concierge mentioned a long-haired young man?'

'I know the district.'

Which amounted to a hint that Maigret and his men had no need to interfere.

'Did you go to his home? Where does he live?'

'In an attic, at the top of a block of flats in the Boulevard Rochechouart. He wasn't there.'

'What time was that?'

'Six o'clock yesterday evening.'

'Had he already taken away his bag?'

'Not yet.'

It had to be admitted that Lognon was the

most persistent of blood-hounds. He had gone off on a trail, not even sure that it was the right one, and had followed it up without losing heart for a moment.

'You were looking for him from six o'clock yesterday until this morning?'

'I know his haunts. He needed money to get away, and he was looking for someone to borrow from. It wasn't till he'd got the money that he went to fetch his bag.'

'How did you find out he was at the Gare du Nord?'

'From a woman who'd seen him take the first bus at the Square d'Anvers. I found him in the waiting-room.'

'And what have you been doing with him since?'

'I took him to the Station to question him.'

'And . . . ?'

'He either knows nothing or won't say anything.'

Maigret had a curious impression that the inspector was in a hurry to get away, and that it wasn't because he wanted to go to bed.

'I suppose I'm to leave him with you?'

'Have you made your report?'

'I'll give it to my inspector this evening.'

'Was it Philippe who supplied the Countess with drugs?'

'Unless it was she who kept him supplied. Anyhow, they were often seen together.'

'Had that been going on long?'

'Several months. If you don't need me any more . . .'

He obviously had something on his mind. Either Philippe had dropped some remark that had set him thinking, or else, during his all-night search, he had come across a clue that he was eager to follow up before other people got on the same track.

Maigret, too, knew the district, and could imagine how Philippe and the Inspector had spent the night. In order to get money, the young man must have been looking up everybody he knew, and he would be looking among the drug addicts. He would have asked the prostitutes lurking at the doors of shady hotels; he would have asked café waiters and night-club porters. Then, as the streets emptied, he would have knocked on the doors of hovels inhabited by degenerates like himself, as seedy and penniless as he was.

Had he succeeded in getting a supply of the drug he wanted? If not, he would fall completely to pieces before long.

'Can I go now?'

'Thank you. You've done a good job.'

'I'm not suggesting he killed the old woman.'

'Neither am I.'

'You're going to hold him?'

'Perhaps.'

Lognon went off, and Maigret opened the door of the inspectors' office. The hold-all was lying on the floor, open. Philippe's face had the colour and general appearance of melted tallow, and whenever anyone moved he raised his arm, as though afraid of being hit.

Not one of the men showed the least pity for him—disgust was written clearly on all their faces.

The bag held only some shabby underwear, a pair of socks, some bottles of medicine—Maigret sniffed at them to make sure they didn't contain heroin—and a few notebooks. He flicked over the pages. They were filled with poems, or to be more exact, with disjointed phrases inspired by the delirium of a drug addict.

'Come in here!' he said.

Philippe slid past him in the attitude of one who expects a kick in the pants. He must be accustomed to them. Even in Montmartre there are people who can't see a fellow like that without hitting him.

Maigret sat down, and left the young man to stand up, sniffing all the time with a dry, exasperating twitch of his nostrils.

'Was the Countess your mistress?'

'She was my protectress,' came the reply, in the mincing tones of a homosexual.

'In other words, you didn't go to bed with her?'

'She was interested in my writing.'

'And gave you money?'

'She helped me to get along.'

'Did she give you a lot?'

'She wasn't rich.'

This was confirmed by the state of his suit, which, though well-cut, was completely threadbare—a blue, double-breasted suit. His shoes must have been given to him, for they were patent leather shoes, more appropriate to evening clothes than to the dirty raincoat he was wearing.

'Why did you try to run away to Belgium?'

The lad did not answer at once, but looked at the door leading into the next office, as though dreading that Maigret would call two tough inspectors to beat him up. Perhaps that had happened to him on previous occasions when he was arrested.

'I've done no harm. I don't understand why I've been arrested.'

'You go with men?'

In his heart of hearts he was proud of it, like all pansies, and an involuntary smile crossed his unnaturally red lips. Maybe he even got a thrill from being pushed about by real men!

'So you won't answer?'

'I have some men friends.'

'But you have women friends too. . . .'

'That's not the same thing.'

'Am I right in supposing that the men provide you with enjoyment and the old ladies with cash?'

'They appreciate my company.'

'Do you know many?'

'Three or four.'

'And they're all your protectresses?'

It took some self-control to speak of such things in an ordinary voice and to look at the lad as though he were a human being.

'They help me sometimes.'

'Do they all take drugs?'

Seeing him turn away his head without replying, Maigret lost his temper. He did not get up, seize the fellow by the filthy collar of his raincoat and shake him; but he rapped out his next words in a metallic voice.

'Listen! I'm not feeling very patient today, and I'm not Lognon. Either you answer my questions at once, or else I'll put you in the cooler for a nice long time. And my inspectors can have a turn at you first.'

'You mean they'll hit me?'

'They'll do whatever they like.'

'They've no right to.'

'And you've no right to hang around spoiling the view. Now, try to answer me. How long had you known the Countess?'

'About six months.'

'Where did you meet her?'

'In a little bar in the Rue Victor-Massé, almost opposite her house.'

'Did you realize at once that she took drugs?'

'It was easy to see.'

'So you sucked up to her?'

'I asked her to give me a little.'

'Had she got any?'

'Yes.'

'A lot?'

'She hardly ever ran short.'

'Do you know how she got it?'

'She didn't tell me.'

'Answer my question. Do you know?'

'I think so.'

'How?'

'From a doctor.'

'A doctor who takes dope himself?'

'Yes.'

'Dr. Bloch?'

'I don't know his name.'

'That's a lie. Ever been to see him?'

'A few times.'

'Why?'

'To get him to give me some.'

'And did he?'

'Only once.'

'Because you threatened to give him away?'

'I had to have some at once. I'd been without for three days. He gave me an injection—just one.'

'Where used you to meet the Countess?'

'In the little bar and at her flat.'

'Why did she give you morphine and money?'

'Because she took an interest in me.'

'I've already warned you that you'd better answer my questions.'

'She was lonely.'

'Hadn't she any friends?'

'She was always alone.'

'You made love to her?'

'I tried to give her pleasure.'

'In her flat?'

'Yes.'

'And you both used to drink red wine?'

'It made me quite sick.'

'And you fell asleep on her bed. Did you ever spend the night there?'

'I stayed as much as two days there.'

'Without ever pulling back the curtains, I bet. Without knowing when it was day and when it was night. Isn't that so?'

After which he doubtless roamed about the streets like a sleep-walker, in a world to which he no longer belonged, looking for another opportunity.

'How old are you?'

'Twenty-eight.'

'When did you begin?'

'Three or four years ago.'

'Why?'

'I don't know.'

'Are you still in touch with your parents?'

'My father washed his hands of me long ago.'

'And your mother?'

'She smuggles a money-order to me now and then.'

'Tell me about the Countess.'

'I don't know anything.'

'Tell me what you do know.'

'She used to be very rich. She was married to a man she didn't love, an old fellow who never gave her a moment's peace and had her trailed by a private detective.'

'Is that what she told you?'

'Yes. He used to get a report every day, describing all she'd said and done, almost minute by minute.'

'Was she already doping herself?'

'No. I don't think so. He died, and everybody tried to grab the money he'd left her.'

126

'Who was "everybody"?'

'All the gigolos on the Riviera, the professional gamblers, her women friends. . . .'

'Did she never mention any names?'

'I don't remember any. You know what it's like. When you've got your load, you talk in a different way. . . .'

Maigret knew this only by hearsay, having never given it a trial.

'She still had some money?'

'Not much. I think she was gradually selling her jewels.'

'Did you ever see them?'

'No.'

'Didn't she trust you?'

'I don't know.'

He was swaying on his legs—they must be skeleton-thin under those loose trousers—to such an extent that Maigret motioned to him to sit down.

'Was there anyone else in Paris besides yourself who was still trying to get money out of her?'

'She never spoke to me about anyone.'

'You never saw anybody in her flat, or talking to her in the street or in a bar?'

Maigret noticed a perceptible hesitation.

'N . . . no!'

He looked sternly at the lad.

'You haven't forgotten what I told you?'

But Philippe had pulled himself together.

'I never saw anyone with her.'

'Neither a man nor a woman?'

'Nobody.'

'Did you ever hear the name "Oscar" mentioned?'

'I don't know anybody of that name.'

'She never seemed to be afraid of anyone?'

'She was only afraid of dying all alone.'

'Did she ever have rows with you?'

The lad's face was too pasty to blush, but a faint pink tinge appeared at the tips of his ears.

'How did you guess?'

He added, with a knowing, slightly contemptuous smile:

'It always ends like that.'

'Explain.'

'Anybody will tell you so.'

That meant, 'anybody who takes drugs.'

Then he added in a dreary tone, as though realizing that he would not be understood:

'When she'd run out of dope and couldn't find any more at once, she'd turn on me, accusing me of having wheedled the stuff out of her, or even of having stolen it—swearing there'd been six or a dozen phials left in the drawer the night before.'

'Had you a key to her flat?'

'No.'

'Did you never go there when she was out?'

'She was hardly ever out. Sometimes she stayed in her room for a week or more on end.'

'Answer my question, yes or no. Did you never go into her flat when she was out?'

Another almost imperceptible hesitation.

'No.'

Maigret muttered as though to himself, without persisting:

'Liar!'

Because of this Philippe, the atmosphere of his own office had become almost as stifling and unreal as that of the flat in the Rue Victor-Massé.

Maigret knew enough about drug addicts to feel certain that now and then, when he was short of dope, Philippe must have tried to get some at all costs. In such a case he would do what he had done the night before, when he was trying to find the money to leave Paris—he would go the round of all his acquaintances, begging shamelessly, all self-respect abandoned.

On the low level where he lived, it must be difficult at times. So he would surely remember that the Countess nearly always had a supply in her drawer, and that if for once she should be reluctant to part with it, he need only wait for her to go out?

This was only a hunch, but it was a logical one.

These people spy on one another, envy one another, steal from one another and sometimes inform on one another. The police are always getting anonymous telephone calls from vengeful characters.

'When did you last see her?'

'The day before yesterday, in the morning.'

'Sure it wasn't yesterday morning?'

'Yesterday morning I was ill and stayed in bed.'

'What was the matter with you?'

'I'd been out of dope for two days.'

'Wouldn't she give you any?'

'She swore she hadn't any, and that the doctor hadn't been able to supply her.'

'Did you quarrel?'

'We were both in a bad temper.'

'Did you believe what she said?'

'She showed me the empty drawer.'

'When did she expect the doctor to come?'

'She didn't know. She'd rung him up and he'd promised to come.'

'You haven't been back there since?'

'No.'

'Now listen. The Countess's body was found yesterday afternoon, about five o'clock. The evening papers were out already. So the news didn't appear till this morning. But you spent the night looking for money so you could get away to Belgium. How did you know the Countess was dead?'

He was obviously about to say:

'I didn't know.'

But the inspector's stony stare made him change his mind.

'I went along the street and saw a crowd on the pavement.'

'What time was that?'

'About half past six.'

Maigret had been in the flat then, and it was true that a policeman had been left at the door to keep out inquisitive idlers.

'Turn out your pockets.'

'Inspector Lognon has made me do that already.'

'Do it again.'

He brought out a dirty handkerchief, two keys on a ring—one was the key of his bag—a penknife, a purse, a little box containing pills, a pocket-book, a notebook, and a hypodermic syringe in its case.

Maigret took the notebook, which was an old one with yellowed pages, full of addresses and telephone numbers. There were hardly any surnames, only initials or Christian names. No mention of an Oscar.

'When you heard the Countess had been strangled, you thought you would be suspected?'

'It's always like that.'

'So you decided to go to Belgium. Do you know anybody there?'

'I've been to Brussels several times.'

'Who gave you the money?'

'A friend—a man.'

'Who?'

'I don't know his name.'

'You'd better tell me.'

'The doctor.'

'Dr. Bloch?'

'Yes. I hadn't found anything. It was three o'clock in the morning and I was beginning to feel scared. Finally I rang him up from a bar in the Rue Caulaincourt.'

'What did you say to him?'

'That I was a friend of the Countess, and that I must have money right away.'

'And he let you have it?'

'I also said that if I were arrested it might be unpleasant for him.'

'In other words, you blackmailed him. Did he tell you to come to his flat?'

'He said if I came to the Rue Victor-Massé, where he lives, he'd be waiting on the pavement.'

'Was that all you asked him for?'

'He gave me a phial of morphine too.'

'And I suppose you gave yourself a shot at once, in some doorway? Is that all you've got to tell me?'

'That's all I know.'

'Is the doctor a homo, too?'

'No.'

'How do you know?'

Philippe shrugged his shoulders, as though the question were too childish to answer.

'Are you hungry?'

'No.'

'Are you thirsty?'

The young man's lips quivered, but it was not food or drink that he needed.

Maigret got up, almost with an effort, and again opened the door into the next office. Torrence happened to be there—a tall, powerful fellow with great beefy hands. Suspects who were interrogated by him would have been surprised to learn that he had a soft heart.

'Come here,' said the inspector. 'You're to shut yourself up with this chap, and not let him out till he's come clean. I don't care whether it takes twenty-four hours or three days. When you're tired, hand over to someone else.'

Philippe protested, wild-eyed.

'I've told you all I know. This is a mean trick. . . .'

Then, shrill-voiced as an angry woman:

'You're a brute! . . . You're horrid! . . . You . . . you . . .'

Maigret stood aside to let him pass, and exchanged a wink with the burly Torrence. The two men went through the inspectors' big office and into a room which was jokingly known as 'the confessional'.

'Have some beer and sandwiches sent up for me!' called Torrence to Lapointe as he went by.

Alone with his assistants, Maigret stretched, shook himself, and refrained with some difficulty from flinging open the window.

'Well, boys?'

Then he noticed that Lucas was back already.

'She's here again, sir, waiting to speak to you.'

'The aunt from Lisieux? Oh yes—how did she behave?'

'Like an old woman who enjoys nothing so much as a funeral. No vinegar or smelling-salts needed. She inspected the body calmly from head to foot. Half-way through, she jumped and asked me:

' "Why have they shaved her?"

'I explained that it wasn't us, and she nearly choked. She showed me the birthmark on the

133

sole of the girl's foot, and said: "You see! But I should have recognized her even without that."

'Then, as we were leaving, she announced, without consulting me:

"I'm going back with you. I have something else to say to the inspector."

'She's in the waiting-room, and I don't think it'll be easy to get rid of her.'

Young Lapointe had just picked up the telephone, and the line seemed to be bad.

'Is that Nice?'

He nodded. Janvier wasn't there. Maigret went back to his office and rang for the usher to bring in the old lady from Lisieux.

'I understand you have something to tell me?'

'I don't know if it will interest you. I was thinking, as I went along. You know how it is. One remembers things, without meaning to. I should not like to be suspected of ill-natured gossiping.'

'Go on, please.'

'It is about Anne-Marie. I told you this morning that she left Lisieux five years ago and that her mother had made no attempt to find out what had become of her—which, between you and me, is a disgraceful way for a mother to behave.'

He would just have to wait; it was no use trying to hurry her.

'There was a lot of talk, of course. Lisieux is a small town, and things always get around in the end. A woman in whom I have every confidence, and who goes once a week to Caen, where she is part owner of a shop, swore to me

134

on her husband's life that not long before Anne-Marie left home she met her at Caen, just going into a doctor's house.'

She paused with a smug expression on her face, and seemed surprised when Maigret asked no question. Then she continued, with a sigh:

'Not just an ordinary doctor—she was going to see Dr. Potut, the gynecologist.'

'In other words, you suspect your niece of having left the town because she was pregnant?'

'That was the rumour, and people wondered who the father could be.'

'Did they find out?'

'Plenty of names were suggested. But I had my own idea, all along, and that's why I came back to see you. It is my duty to help you discover the truth, is it not?'

She was beginning to feel that the police were not as inquisitive as people made out; for Maigret wasn't helping her at all. Far from urging her to speak, he was listening as indifferently as an old father-confessor, dozing behind the latticed partition of his box.

She went on, as though making a most important disclosure:

'Anne-Marie's throat was always weak. She used to get tonsillitis at least once every winter, and when her tonsils were removed it made no difference. That year, I remember, my sister-in-law had decided to take her to La Bourboule for treatment—that's the great place for throat illnesses.'

Maigret remembered that Arlette's voice had

been slightly hoarse; he had put it down to drink, smoking, and sleepless nights.

'When she left Lisieux she can't have been pregnant for more than three or four months, because it didn't show. That's the utmost it can have been, especially as she always wore very tight-fitting dresses. Well, that exactly fits in with her visit to La Bourboule! I am perfectly certain it was there that she met the man by whom she became pregnant, and she most likely went off to join him. If it had been a Lisieux man, he would either have arranged for an abortion or gone away with her.'

Maigret slowly lit his pipe. He was aching all over, as though from a long tramp; but it was disgust that caused it. He was tempted to go and open the window, just as when Philippe had been there.

'You're going back to Lisieux, I suppose?'

'Not today. I have friends in Paris and shall probably spend a few days with them. I will leave you their address.'

The friends lived near the Boulevard Pasteur. She had already written out the address, on the back of one of her visiting cards, and added the telephone number.

'Don't hesitate to ring up if you need me.'

'Thank you.'

'I shall always be ready to help.'

'I am sure you will.'

He conducted her to the door, without a smile, closed it slowly behind her, stretched himself

and rubbed his head with both hands, groaning
in a low voice:

'What a filthy lot!'

'May I come in, sir?'

It was Lapointe. He had a sheet of paper in
his hand and looked much excited.

'Did you phone for beer?'

'The waiter from the Brasserie Dauphine has
just come up with the tray.'

The beer had not yet been taken to Torrence
in his retreat, and Maigret, seizing the glass,
swallowed its cool, frothy contents in one long
draught.

'Ring up and tell them to send round some
more!'

7

LAPOINTE said, not without a faint touch of
jealousy in his voice: 'I'm beginning by giving
you "best regards from little Julien". I was told
you'd understand.'

'Is he at Nice?'

'He was moved there from Limoges a few
weeks ago.'

Julien was the son of an old inspector who
had worked with Maigret for a long time and
gone to live on the Riviera when he retired. As
luck would have it, Maigret had hardly seen the
boy since the days when he used to give him
rides on his knee.

'It was he who spoke to me on the telephone
yesterday,' went on Lapointe, 'and I've been in
touch with him ever since. When he knew it was
you who'd told me to ring up, and that it was
really you he was to work for, he got tremen-

dously excited and went all out at the job. He's been spending hours in an attic at the police station, hunting through old records. It seems there are any number of parcels, full of reports on cases everybody's completely forgotten. They're thrown about in an awful mess, and the pile nearly reaches the ceiling.'

'Did he find the report on the Farnheim business?'

'He's just been giving me the list of the witnesses who were questioned after the Count's death. I'd asked him to make a special effort to find the names of the servants who were employed at The Oasis. Here they are:

'*Antoinette Méjat, aged nineteen, housemaid,*

'*Rosalie Moncoeur, aged fory-two, cook,*

'*Maria Pinaco, aged twenty-three, kitchen-maid,*

'*Angelino Luppin, aged thirty-eight, butler.*'

Maigret waited, standing by the window of his office, watching the snow, which was falling less thickly now. Lapointe continued, after a dramatic pause:

'*Oscar Bonvoisin, aged thirty-five, valet-chauffeur.*'

'An Oscar!' observed the inspector. 'I suppose nobody knows what's become of all these people?'

'Well, Inspector Julien had an idea. It isn't long since he came to Nice, and he'd been struck by the number of wealthy foreigners who come to spend a few months there, rent biggish houses and do a lot of entertaining. It occurred to him that they must need servants at very short notice. And he found an employment bureau which specializes in staffing big houses.

'It's kept by an old lady who's been there for over twenty years. She doesn't remember Count von Farnheim, or the Countess, or Oscar Bonvoisin: but not more than a year ago she found a job for Rosalie Moncoeur, the cook who's one of her regulars, with some South Americans who have a villa at Nice and spend part of the year in Paris. I have their address—132, Avenue d'Iéna. The old lady thought they were in Paris now.'

'Anything known about the others?'

'Julien's still following that up. Shall I go and see her, sir?'

Maigret almost agreed, to please Lapointe, who was burning with eagerness to question the Farnheims' ex-cook. But he finally declared that he would go himself—chiefly, to be quite honest, because he wanted to get some fresh air, have another beer on his way, and escape from his office, where he felt stifled that morning.

'Meantime, you look through the registers and see if there's anything under "Bonvoisin". You'll have to hunt through the police forms of the lodging-houses too. And ring up all the town halls and police stations in Paris.'

'Very well, sir.'

Poor Lapointe! Maigret felt sorry for him, but not to the extent of giving up his outing.

Before he left, he looked into the little room where Torrence and Philippe were shut up together. Torrence had taken his coat off, but even so there were beads of sweat on his forehead. Philippe, perched on the edge of a chair, was as white as a sheet and appeared likely to faint at any moment.

Maigret had no need to ask any questions. He knew Torrence would never give up—that he would go on with the little game till night came—and right through the night if necessary.

Less than half an hour later, a taxi pulled up outside a solemn-looking building in the Avenue d'Iéna, and the inspector walked into a marble-pillared hall, where he was greeted by a porter in a dark uniform. He explained his identity, asked whether Rosalie Moncoeur was still working in the house, and was directed towards the back-stairs.

'It's on the third floor.'

He had drunk two more beers on his way and got rid of his headache. The staircase was a narrow, spiral one, and he counted the floors in an undertone as he went up. He rang the bell at a brown-painted door. A stout, white-haired woman opened it and looked at him in astonishment.

'Madame Moncoeur?'

'What do you want with her?'

'To speak to her.'

'It's me.'

She was busy at her stove, and a swarthy little girl was putting a delicious-smelling mixture through a sieve.

'I believe you worked at one time for Count and Countess von Farnheim?'

'Who are you?'

'I come from the Judicial Police.'

'You don't mean to tell me you're digging up that old story?'

'Not exactly. Did you know the Countess was dead?'

'It happens to everyone. No, I didn't know.'

'It was in the papers this morning.'

'Do you suppose I read the papers! With fifteen or twenty people coming to dinner here almost every day!'

'She was murdered.'

'That's funny.'

'Why does it strike you as funny?'

She had not asked him to sit down, and now went on with her work, talking to him as she might to a tradesman. She was obviously a woman of experience, not easily impressed.

'I don't know what made me say that. Who killed her?'

'We don't know yet, and that's what I'm trying to find out. Did you keep on working for her after her husband's death?'

'Only for a couple of weeks. We didn't get on.'

'Why not?'

Rosalie looked to see how the kitchen-maid was managing, and then opened the oven to baste a fowl.

'Because it wasn't the kind of work for me.'

'You mean it wasn't a respectable house?'

'Put it that way if you like. I'm fond of my work, and I expect people to come to meals at the right time and in a state to know more or less what they're eating. That'll do, Irma. Take the hard-boiled eggs out of the refrigerator and separate the yolks from the whites.'

She opened a bottle of Madeira and poured a liberal quantity into a sauce which she was stirring slowly with a wooden spoon.

'You remember Oscar Bonvoisin?'

She looked at him then, as though on the point of saying:

'So that's what you were getting at!'

But she remained silent.

'You heard what I asked?'

'I'm not deaf.'

'What kind of man was he?'

'A valet.'

As Maigret looked surprised at her tone, she added:

'I don't like valets. They're all bone-idle. Specially when they're chauffeurs as well. They think they're cock of the roost, and put on worse airs than the master and mistress.'

'Was Bonvoisin like that?'

'I don't remember his surname. He was always called Oscar.'

'What did he look like?'

'He was a good-looking fellow, and knew it. At least, some women admire that sort. I don't myself, and I let him know it.'

'He made love to you?'

'In his way.'

'Meaning——?'

'Why are you asking me all this?'

'Because I need to know.'

'You think he may have killed the Countess?'

'It's possible.'

Irma was more excited by this conversation than either of the participants—she was so thrilled at being almost mixed up in a real crime that she had quite forgotten what she was supposed to be doing.

'Well, Irma? What about mashing up those yolks?'

'Can you give me a description of him?'

'As he was in those days, yes. But I don't know what he looks like now.'

At that moment Maigret saw a gleam in her eyes, and he said quickly:

'Are you sure? You've never seen him since?'

'That's just what I was wondering. I'm not sure. A few weeks ago I went to see my brother, who has a small café, and in the street I met a man I thought I knew. He looked hard at me, too, as though he was searching his memory. And then, suddenly, I had the impression he'd begun to walk very fast, turning away his face.'

'And you thought it was Oscar?'

'Not at the moment. Later on I had the vague idea, and now I'd almost swear it was him.'

'Where's your brother's café?'

'In the Rue Caulaincourt.'

'And it was in Montmartre that you met this man you thought you recognized?'

'Just at the corner of the Place Clichy.'

'Now try to tell me what kind of man he was.'

'I don't like giving people away.'

'You'd rather let a murderer go free?'

'If he's only killed the Countess he's done no great harm.'

'If he's killed her, he's killed at least one other woman and there's no reason to suppose that he'll stop there.'

She shrugged her shoulders.

'Oh well, it's his look-out, after all. He wasn't tall. Rather on the small side. It made him so cross that he used to wear high heels, like a woman, to make himself look taller. I used to tease him about it, and he'd scowl at me without saying a word.'

'He wasn't very talkative?'

'He was as close as any oyster—never said what he was doing or what he thought. He was very dark, with hair that grew thick down to a low forehead, and bushy black eyebrows. Some women thought his eyes had an irresistible expression. Not me. He'd stare at you, looking as pleased with himself as if he'd been the only man in the world, and you were just dirt.'

'Go on.'

Now that she was launched, she showed no hesitation. All the time she talked, she was bustling about the kitchen, which was full of delicious smells, juggling deftly, as it were, with pans and gadgets, and glancing every few minutes at the electric clock.

'Antoinette fell for him—she was crazy about him. So was Maria.'

'You mean the housemaid and the kitchen-maid?'

'Yes. And others who worked there before them. Servants never stayed long in that house. You never knew whether to take your orders from the old man or from the Countess. You see what I mean? Oscar didn't make love to the servants, as you said a minute ago. As soon as he saw a new one, he just stared at her as though he was taking possession of her.

'Then, the first evening, he'd go upstairs and into her room as though it was all arranged beforehand.'

'Some men are like that—they believe no woman can resist them.'

'Antoinette cried her eyes out.'

'Why?'

'Because she was really in love with him, and hoped for a time that he'd marry her. But once he'd had enough he'd go away without a word. And after that he'd take no more notice of them. Never say anything pleasant or pay them the slightest attention. Until he was in the mood again, and then back he'd go to one of their rooms.

'Anyhow, he had all the women he wanted, and not only servants.'

'You think he had an affair with the Countess?'

'Before the Count had been dead two days.'

'How do you know?'

'Because I saw him come out of her room at six in the morning. That was partly why I left. When the servants begin to share the best bedroom, it's the last straw.'

'Was he getting above himself?'

'He was doing just as he liked. You could feel there was nobody giving him orders any more.'

'Did it never occur to you that the Count might have been murdered?'

'It was none of my business.'

'But it did occur to you?'

'It occurred to the police too, didn't it? Else why did they ask us all those questions?'

'It might have been Oscar?'

'I don't say that. She was probably just as capable of doing it herself.'

'Did you go on working at Nice?'

'At Nice and Monte Carlo. I like the climate down there, and I've only come to Paris accidentally, to please my employers.'

'You never heard any more about the Countess?'

'I saw her go past once or twice, but we didn't lead the same kind of life.'

'And Oscar?'

'I never saw him again in those parts. I don't think he stayed on the Riviera.'

'But you think you caught sight of him a few weeks ago. What did he look like?'

'All you policemen seem to think that whenever one passes a man in the street one notices everything about him.'

'Had he aged much?'

'He's like me—fifteen years older than he was.'

'That means he's in his fifties.'

'I'm nearly ten years older than he is. Another three or four years in service, and then I'll retire to a little house I've bought at Cagnes and cook only for myself. Fried eggs and cutlets.'

'You don't remember how he was dressed?'

'In the Place Clichy?'

'Yes.'

'In rather dark clothes. I don't say black, but dark. He had a heavy overcoat on, and gloves. I noticed the gloves. He was very smart.'

'What about his hair?'

'A man doesn't go round carrying his hat, in the middle of winter.'

'Was it grey at the temples?'

'I think so. But that wasn't what struck me.'

'What did?'

'He'd got fatter. He was always broad-shouldered. Used to go around naked to the waist whenever he could, because he had tremendous muscles, and some women found that attractive. He didn't look so powerful when he had his clothes on. Now—if it was him I met—he looks rather like a bull. His neck's thicker, and he seems even shorter than he used to.'

'You never heard any more of Antoinette?'

'She died. Not long afterwards.'

'What of?

'A miscarriage. At least that's what I was told.'

'And Maria Pinaco?'

'I don't know if she's still at it, but last time I

saw her she had her stretch on the Cours Albert-Premier, at Nice.'

'Was that long ago?'

'Two years, or a bit more.'

She did have the curiosity to ask him:

'How was the Countess killed?'

'Strangled.'

She made no comment, but looked as though she thought that sounded quite like Oscar's way.

'And who was the other woman?'

'A girl you're not likely to have known—she was only twenty years old.'

'Nice of you to remind me that I'm an old woman.'

'That's not what I meant. She came from Lisieux, and there's nothing to suggest that she ever lived on the Riviera. All I know is that she once visited La Bourboule.'

'Near Le Mont-Dore?'

'In Auvergne—yes.'

She looked at Maigret with thoughtful eyes.

'Well, once I've begun to give him away . . .' she muttered. 'Oscar came from the Auvergne,' she went on. 'I don't know exactly what part, but he had a bit of an accent, and when I wanted to annoy him I'd imitate it. He'd go pale with rage. And now, if you'll excuse me, I'll ask you to clear out, because it's only half an hour to lunch-time, and I need the kitchen to myself.'

'I may be back to see you again.'

'Well, so long as you give no more trouble than you have today. . . ! What's your name?'

'Maigret.'

The kitchen-maid jumped—evidently she read the papers—but the cook had obviously never heard of him.

'I shall remember that, because it means "thin" and you're rather on the fat side. Now I come to think of it, Oscar's about your build, these days, but a head shorter. You see what I mean?'

'Thank you very much.'

'Not at all. Only if you arrest him, I'd prefer not to be called as a witness. Never does you any good, when you're in service. Besides, those lawyers ask a lot of questions to try and make a fool of you. It happened to me once, and I swore it shouldn't happen again. So don't count on me.'

She showed him calmly out of the door, and he had to walk the whole length of the Avenue before finding a taxi. Instead of going to the Quai des Orfèvres, he went home to lunch. He got back to the office about half past two; the snow had quite stopped by then, and the streets were covered with a thin layer of blackish, greasy mud.

When he opened the door of the 'confessional' he found it was blue with smoke, and there were about twenty cigarette-ends in the ashtray. It was Torrence who had smoked them, for Philippe was not a smoker. There was a tray there too, with the remains of some sandwiches, and five empty beer glasses.

'Would you come outside for a moment?'

Emerging into the outer office, Torrence mopped his forehead and relaxed, sighing:

'That chap's wearing me out. He's like a wet rag—nothing to get hold of. Twice I thought he was going to come clean. I'm sure he's got something to say. He seems to be at the end of his tether—looks at you with imploring eyes—and then, at the last second, he changes his mind and swears he doesn't know a thing. It makes me sick. Just now he drove me so far that I slapped him in the face with the flat of my hand. Do you know what he did?'

Maigret said nothing.

'He put his hand to his cheek and began snivelling, as though he was talking to another pansy like himself: "You're very unkind!" I mustn't do that again, because I bet it gives him a thrill.'

Maigret couldn't help smiling.

'Am I to go on?'

'Have another shot. We'll try something else presently, perhaps. Has he had anything to eat?'

'He nibbled daintily at a sandwich, with his little finger crooked in the air. You can see he's missing his dope. If I promised him some, he might begin to talk. The narcotics people must have some, don't you think?'

'I'll mention it to the Chief. But don't do anything about it yet. Just keep on with your questions.'

Torrence gave a glance round at his familiar surroundings, drew a deep breath of air, and went back again into the depressing atmosphere of the 'confessional'.

'Anything fresh, Lapointe?' asked Maigret.

Lapointe had hardly put down the telephone

since his arrival that morning and, like Torrence, had lunched on a sandwich and a glass of beer.

'About a dozen Bonvoisins, but not one of them's an Oscar.'

'Try to get a call through to La Bourboule. You may have better luck there.'

'Have you got a tip?'

'Perhaps.'

'From the cook?'

'She thinks she met him quite lately in Paris —and better still, in Montmartre.'

'Why La Bourboule?'

'For one thing, he comes from that district, and for another thing, Arlette seems to have had an eventful meeting with someone or other down there, five years ago.'

Maigret spoke without much conviction.

'No news of Lognon?' he went on.

He rang up the police station in the Rue de La Rochefoucauld himself, but was told that Inspector Lognon had only looked in for a moment.

'He said he was working for you and would be out all day.'

For the next fifteen minutes, Maigret paced to and fro in his office, smoking his pipe. Then he seemed to reach a decision, and went for an interview with his chief.

'What's the news, Maigret?' he was asked. 'Why weren't you in to hear the report this morning?'

'I was asleep,' he confessed frankly.

'Have you seen the afternoon papers?'

Maigret indicated by a gesture that these did not interest him.

'They're wondering whether any more women are going to be strangled.'

'I don't think so.'

'Why not?'

'Because the man who killed the Countess and Arlette isn't a lunatic. On the contrary, he knows exactly what he's about.'

'Have you identified him?'

'Perhaps. Probably, in fact.'

'D'you expect to arrest him today?'

'We have to discover where he hangs out, and I haven't the faintest idea about that, except that it's more than likely to be in Montmartre. There's only one circumstance in which there might be another victim.'

'What's that?'

'If Arlette talked to anybody else—for instance, to Betty or Tania, the other women at Picratt's.'

'Have you asked them?'

'They don't say a word. Neither does Fred, the proprietor, neither does the Grasshopper. And neither does that unhealthy worm, Philippe, although he's been questioned all morning. And he, at least, knows something, I'll be bound. He used to be always seeing the Countess. It was she who supplied him with morphine.'

'Where did she get it?'

'Through her doctor.'

'You've arrested him?'

'Not yet. That's a job for the narcotics people. I've been wondering for the last hour whether I ought to take a risk, or not.'

'What risk?'

'The risk of being landed with another corpse. That's what I want your advice about. It's more than probable that this chap Bonvoisin killed both women, and I've no doubt we can lay hands on him by routine methods. But that may take days, or weeks. It's largely a matter of luck. And unless I'm much mistaken, he's no fool. Before we catch him he may bump off someone else— or several other people—for knowing too much.'

'What's the risk you want to take?'

'I didn't say I wanted to.'

The Chief smiled.

'Explain, please.'

'If Philippe knows something, as I'm convinced he does, Oscar must be feeling very uneasy. I need only tell the press that Philippe has been questioned for several hours with no result, and then let him go.'

'I'm beginning to understand.'

'The first possibility is that Philippe will go straight to Oscar, but I'm not really counting on that. Unless it's his only way of getting dope— he's beginning to need it very badly.'

'And the other possibility?'

The Chief had already guessed what it was.

'You see the notion. A drug addict can't be trusted. Philippe's said nothing yet, but that doesn't mean he'll keep quiet for ever, and Oscar knows it.'

154

'So he'll try to get rid of him.'

'That's it! I didn't want to make the experiment without consulting you.'

'D'you think you can prevent him from killing the boy?'

'I shall take every precaution. Bonvoisin isn't the man to use a gun. Guns make too much noise, and he doesn't seem to like noise.'

'When do you propose to let your witness go?'

'At dusk. It'll be easier to keep a discreet watch over him then. I'll put as many men as necessary on his tail. And after all, if there should be an accident I don't feel it would be any great loss.'

'I'd rather there wasn't one.'

'So would I.'

There was a moment's silence, and then the Chief said with a sigh:

'I leave it to you, Maigret. Good luck.'

*

'You were quite right, sir.'

'About what?'

Lapointe was so glad to be playing an important part in an investigation, that he had almost forgotten Arlette's death.

'I got the information at once. Oscar Bonvoisin was born at Le Mont-Dore, where his father was a hotel porter and his mother a chambermaid in the same hotel. He had his first job there, as a page boy. Then he left the district and didn't come back till about ten years ago—when he bought a house, not at Le Mont-Dore, but nearby, outside La Bourboule.'

'Does he usually live there?'

'No. He spends part of the summer there, and sometimes a few days in the winter.'

'He isn't married?'

'No—a bachelor. His mother's still alive.'

'Living in his house?'

'No. She has a small flat in the town. It's thought that he supports her. He's supposed to have made a good deal of money and to be doing some very big business in Paris.'

'The description?'

'Fits with what we've got.'

'Would you like to take on a confidential job?'

'You know I would, sir.'

'Even if it's pretty risky and means a lot of responsibility?'

His love for Arlette must have come surging back, for he said a little too ardently:

'I don't care if I'm killed.'

'Right! It's not a question of being killed, but of seeing that someone else isn't. And it's essential for you not to look like a police inspector.'

'You think I generally look like one?'

'Go to the wardrobe room and pick yourself out something suitable for an unemployed man who's looking for work and hoping not to find any. Take a cap rather than a hat. And be careful not to overdo it.'

Janvier was back, and Maigret gave him very similar instructions.

'You're to look like a clerk going home from work.'

156

Then he chose two inspectors whom Philippe had never seen.

He called the four men into his office, spread out a plan of Montmartre, and explained what they were to do.

Dusk was falling fast. The lamps on the quay and up the Boulevard Saint-Michel were already lit.

Maigret was reluctant to wait for complete darkness, but it would be more difficult to follow Philippe without attracting his attention—and Bonvoisin's, which was more important—in the deserted streets, before the night life of Montmartre began.

'Would you come here for a moment, Torrence?'

Torrence emerged, to declare furiously:

'I give it up! He makes me spew, that lad does! Anyone else can try who's got a strong stomach, but as for me . . .'

'You'll have finished in five minutes.'

'We're to let him go?'

'As soon as the last edition of the evening papers is out.'

'What have the papers got to do with him?'

'They'll announce that he's been questioned for hours, with no result.'

'I see.'

'Go and shake him up a bit more. Then put his hat on his head and push him out, telling him he'd better behave himself.'

'Do I give him back his syringe?'

'His syringe and his money.'

Torrence looked at the four waiting inspectors.

'Is that why they're all dolled up for a fancy-dress ball?'

One of the four went to look for a taxi, in which he was to wait quietly near the entrance to police headquarters. The others set out for certain strategic points.

Meanwhile, Maigret had found time to ring up the 'narcotics squad' and the police station in the Rue de La Rochefoucauld.

Torrence had purposely left the door of the 'confessional' ajar, and his thunderous voice could be heard at full pitch, as he told Philippe exactly what he thought of him.

'I wouldn't even touch you with a barge-pole, d'you understand?' he roared. 'I'd be afraid of giving you the wrong idea. And now it's time I had this office disinfected. Take what you call your overcoat. Put your hat on.'

'You mean I can go?'

'I mean I'm sick of the sight of you—we all are. You're more than we can stand—is that clear? Pick up your rubbish and get out, you filthy rat!'

'There's no need to jostle me.'

'I'm not jostling you.'

'You're shouting at me. . . .'

'Get out!'

'I'm going. . . . I'm going. . . . Thank you.'

A door opened, and banged shut. At this hour

the corridor was deserted, and only two or three people were waiting in the badly-lit ante-room.

Philippe made his way down the long, dusty passage, where he looked like an insect hunting for its way out.

Maigret, who was watching him through the crack of his own door, saw him at last reach the stairs and begin to descend.

All the same, he felt a little remorseful. He shut the door and looked at Torrence, who was stretching himself like an actor who has just got back to his dressing-room. Torrence could see that he was worried and thoughtful.

'You think he'll get himself bumped off?'

'What I'm hoping is that the attempt will be made, but won't succeed.'

'The first thing he'll do will be to rush to where he thinks he can find morphia.'

'Yes.'

Do you know where?'

'To Dr. Bloch.'

'Will he give him any?'

'I sent him a message to forbid him to, and he won't dare.'

'So what?'

'I don't know. I'm going up to Montmartre. The men know where to find me. You stay here. If anything turns up, phone me at Picratt's.'

'That means more delicious sandwiches for me. Never mind—I shan't be sharing them with that pansy this time!'

Maigret put on his hat and coat, chose two

empty pipes from the selection on his desk and put them in his pockets.

Before taking a taxi to the Rue Pigalle, he called in at the Brasserie Dauphine for a brandy. He had lost his hangover, but began to suspect that he was in for another next morning.

8

ARLETTE's photographs had at last been removed from the showcase. Instead, there were those of another girl, who had taken her place and was to do the same act, perhaps even in the same dress. But Betty was right, it was a difficult business. The girl was young and plump, probably pretty; but even in the photo, her gesture of beginning to undress had a provocative vulgarity which was reminiscent of an indecent postcard, or of one of the clumsily-painted nudes that undulate on the canvas-sided booths of fairgrounds.

The door opened at a push and Maigret went in. A lamp was burning above the bar and another at the far end of the room, with a long stretch of dimness between the two. Right at the back of the room was Fred, in a white, polo-necked sweater, with big horn spectacles on his nose, reading the evening paper.

The Alfonsis' upstairs quarters were so cramped that in the day-time they probably used the cabaret as a dining-room and sitting-room. Very likely some of the regular customers, who were more like personal friends, came in for a drink at the bar at *apéritif* time.

Fred looked across the top of his glasses at Maigret advancing towards him and, without getting up, held out a fat hand and motioned him to sit down.

'I was expecting you,' he said.

He didn't explain why, and Maigret didn't ask. Fred finished reading his article on the case, took off his spectacles, and inquired:

'What will you take? A brandy?'

He went to the bar, poured out two glasses, and returned to his seat with the contented sigh of a man glad to be at home. Steps could be heard overhead.

'Is your wife up there?' asked the inspector.

'Yes—giving a lesson to the new girl.'

Maigret repressed a smile at the thought of fat Rose giving a lesson in the art of strip-tease.

'Doesn't it interest you?' he asked Fred, who answered with a shrug:

'She's a pretty kid. Her breasts are better than Arlette's and her skin's clearer. But it's not the same thing.'

'Why did you make out to me that you'd never been with Arlette except in the kitchen?'

Fred showed no embarrassment.

'You've been questioning the hotel-keepers? I had to tell you that, because of my wife. No sense in hurting her feelings unnecessarily. She's always afraid I'll leave her one day for a younger woman.'

'You wouldn't have left her for Arlette?'

Fred looked Maigret straight in the eyes.

'For her, yes, if she'd asked me to.'

'You'd really fallen for her?'

'Call it how you like. I've had hundreds of women in my life, probably thousands. I've never bothered to count 'em. But I've never known another like her.'

'Did you suggest she should settle down with you?'

'I gave her to understand that it wouldn't displease me, and that she'd do quite well out of it.'

'And she refused?'

Fred sighed, raised his glass, gazed through it for a moment and then took a sip.

'If she hadn't refused, she'd probably be alive now. You know as well as I do that she had a man somewhere. How he kept his hold on her, I never found out.'

'You tried?'

'I even trailed her sometimes.'

'With no result?'

'She was too smart for me. What's your game with the pansy?'

'You know Philippe?'

'No. But I know others like him. Now and

then one of 'em ventures in here, but I don't encourage them. D'you suppose it'll lead to anything?'

It was Maigret's turn to reply by silence. Fred had understood, of course. He was practically in the same line of business—the two of them worked with much the same material, only in a different way and for different reasons.

'There are certain things you didn't tell me about Arlette,' remarked the inspector gently.

Fred gave a slight smile.

'You've guessed what they were?' he inquired.

'I've guessed what kind they were.'

'May as well take the opportunity, while my wife's still upstairs. Although the kid's dead, I prefer not to talk too much about her in front of Rose. Between you and me, I'll probably never leave the old girl. We're so used to each other, I couldn't get along without her. Even if I'd gone away with Arlette I'd most likely have come back.'

The telephone began to ring. There was no call-box—the instrument was in the cloakroom, and Maigret went towards it, saying:

'That'll be for me.'

He was right. It was Lapointe.

'It's just as you said, sir. He went straight to Dr. Bloch's house, by bus. He was only in there for a very few minutes and when he came out he was a bit paler than before. Now he's making for the Place Blanche.'

'Everything all right?'

'Everything's all right. Don't worry.'

Maigret went back to his seat, and Fred asked no questions.

'You were telling me about Arlette.'

'I'd always thought she was a girl from a good family, who'd left home for some whim. Matter of fact, it was Rose who called my attention to some points I hadn't noticed. And I rather think she was younger than she made out. She'd probably swapped identity cards with an older friend.'

Fred spoke slowly, like a man pondering over pleasant memories, while Maigret's gaze followed his, down the long dusky funnel of the narrow room, to where the polished mahogany of the bar beside the door gleamed in the lamplight.

'It's hard to explain what I mean. Some girls have an instinct for love-making, and I've come across virgins who were hotter than any old pro. But Arlette was different.

'I don't know the fellow who taught her her stuff, but I take off my hat to him. As I told you before, I'm an authority on the subject, but I assure you I've never come across a woman who was her equal. He'd not only taught her as much as I knew, but some tricks I didn't know as well. At my age, just imagine! And with the life I've led! I was staggered.

'And she enjoyed doing it, that I'd swear. Not only going to bed with anybody and everybody, but even her act; such a pity you didn't see that.

'I've known women of thirty-five or forty, most of them a bit cracked, who found it amusing to lead men on. I've known young girls who liked

playing with fire. But they were never like her
—they never went at it so purposefully.

'I know I'm not explaining it properly, but I
can't describe exactly what I mean.

'You asked me about a fellow called Oscar. I
don't know if there is such a person, or who he
is. But what's certain is that Arlette was in some-
body's hands, and that he had a firm hold on
her. Do you suppose she suddenly felt sick of
him and decided to give him away?'

'When she went to the police station in the
Rue La Rochefoucauld at four o'clock yesterday
morning, she knew a crime was to be committed, and that it involved a Countess.'

'But why did she pretend she'd found it out
here, by listening to a conversation between two
men?'

'To begin with, she was drunk. That was probably what made her decide to take the step.'

'Unless she drank to screw up her courage to
the right point?'

'I wonder,' murmured Maigret, 'if the way she
behaved with young Albert . . .'

'Oh, by the way, I've discovered he's one of
your inspectors!'

'I didn't know it myself at first. He was genuinely in love.'

'I noticed that.'

'There's a romantic streak in every woman.
He was urging her to change her way of life.
She could have had a husband if she wanted.'

'And you think that made her fed up with
Oscar?'

'At any rate she felt restive at one moment, and went to the police station. But even then she didn't want to say too much. She left him a chance to get away with it, by giving only a vague description and a Christian name.'

'A mean trick all the same, don't you think?'

'Once faced with the police, she may have regretted her idea. She was surprised at being kept there, and at being sent to the Quai des Orfèvres, and she'd had time to sleep off her champagne. So then she was much less definite—came near to declaring she'd made it all up.'

'That's just like a woman,' nodded Fred. 'What puzzles me is how the chap found out. Because he was already waiting for her when she got back home.'

Maigret stared silently at his pipe.

'I bet you thought I knew him and wouldn't admit it,' went on Fred.

'Perhaps.'

'At one moment you even thought it might be me.'

It was Maigret's turn to smile at this.

'In fact I've been wondering,' continued the other, 'whether it wasn't on purpose that she gave a description that sounded a bit like me— just because her man is quite different.'

'No. The description was correct.'

'D'you know the fellow?'

'His name's Oscar Bonvoisin.'

Fred showed no reaction. The name was evidently unknown to him.

'Well, he's no fool!' he exclaimed. 'Whoever he may be, I take off my hat to him. I thought I knew Montmartre inside out. I've talked it over with the Grasshopper, who's always rooting about in corners. Arlette had been working here for two years. She lived only a few hundred yards away. As I've told you, I followed her more than once, because I was curious. So don't you find it extraordinary that we should know nothing about this fellow?'

He flicked at the paper spread out on the table.

'What's more, he was in with that crazy old Countess. Women like that don't go around unnoticed. They belong to a separate world, where everybody knows everybody, more or less. And yet your men seem to be as much in the dark as I am. Lognon dropped in a while ago and tried to pick my brains, but there weren't any pickings.'

The telephone rang again.

'Is that you, sir? I'm speaking from the Boulevard de Clichy. He's just gone into the restaurant at the corner of the Rue Lepic and been round to all the tables, as though looking for someone. He looked disappointed. There's another restaurant next door, and he began by pressing his nose against the window. Then he went in, and through to the cloakroom. Janvier went in afterwards, and questioned the attendant. She said he'd asked whether a man called Bernard had left a message for him.'

'Did she say who Bernard was?'

'She made out she didn't know.'

He must be a drug-peddler, of course.

'Philippe's going towards the Place Clichy now.'

Maigret had scarcely hung up when the phone rang again, and this time it was Torrence.

'I say, sir, when I went back to the "confessional" to open the window, I fell over young Philippe's bag. We forgot to give it back to him. Do you suppose he'll come to fetch it?'

'Not before he's found some dope.'

Returning to the main room, Maigret found Madame Rose and Arlette's successor both there, on the dance-floor. Fred had moved into one of the boxes, and was sitting there like a customer. He signed to Maigret to do the same.

'Rehearsal!' he announced with a wink.

The girl was very young, with fair, fuzzy hair and the pink complexion of a baby or a country lass—whose firm limbs and artless expression she had as well.

'Shall I begin?' she asked.

There was no music and no spotlight. Fred merely switched on one more lamp, above the dance-floor, and began to hum the tune that usually went with Arlette's act, beating time with his hand.

Rose, after greeting Maigret, started gesticulating at the girl, to show her what she had to do.

The newcomer broke awkwardly into what was intended as a dance step, swaying her hips as much as possible; and then began, slowly, as she had been taught, to undo the hooks on the long black sheath she was wearing, which had been let out to fit her.

Fred cast an eloquent glance at the inspector. Neither of them laughed, though they could hardly keep from smiling. The girl's shoulders were revealed, and then one breast, which, in this humdrum atmosphere, caused a kind of surprise.

Rose held up her hand for a pause at this point, and the girl stared fixedly at it.

'Go right round the floor now,' said Fred, resuming his humming at once. 'Not so quick. . . . Tra-la-la-la. . . . Good! . . .'

And Rose's hand indicated:

'The other breast. . . .'

Her nipples were large and pink. The dress slid slowly down, the shadow of the navel appeared, and finally the girl, with a clumsy gesture, let it fall right to the ground and stood there on the dance-floor, hands clasped over her nakedness.

'That'll do for today,' sighed Fred. 'You can go and put your clothes on again, my child.'

The girl picked up the dress and went off to the kitchen. Rose came to sit with the men for a moment.

'They'll have to be satisfied with that! It's the best I can get out of her. She does it the way she'd drink a cup of coffee. It's nice of you to come and see us, Inspector.'

She meant it, she really was pleased to see him.

'Do you think you'll find the murderer?'

'Monsieur Maigret hopes to catch him to-night,' said her husband.

She glanced from one to the other, decided she was in the way, and went off to the kitchen in her turn, announcing:

'I'm going to get some food ready. You'll have something with us, Inspector?'

He did not refuse. He didn't know yet whether he would. He had chosen Picratt's as a strategic point and also, a little, because he liked being there. He wondered whether it wasn't the atmosphere of the place that had made young Lapointe fall in love with Arlette.

Fred went to turn off the lamps over the dance-floor. They heard the girl walking about overhead. Then she came down and joined Rose in the kitchen.

'What were we saying?'

'We were talking about Oscar.'

'I suppose you've made inquiries in all the cheap hotels?'

The question was not worth an answer.

'And he never went to Arlette's place either?'

They had reached the same point, because they both knew the district and the kind of life that went on there.

If Oscar and Arlette had been on intimate terms, they obviously must have had some meeting-place.

'Did no one ever ring her up here?' asked Maigret.

'I didn't pay attention, but if it had happened often I should have noticed.'

And she had no telephone in her flat. According to the concierge, no men ever came there—and that concierge was reliable, not like the one in the Countess's house.

Lapointe had been all through the registration slips of the cheap hotels. Janvier had been the round of the places themselves, and done it thoroughly, for he'd come across Fred's traces.

It was more than twenty-four hours since Arlette's photo had appeared in the papers, and nobody had so far reported having seen her go regularly into any particular place.

'I tell you again, he's no fool, that chap!'

Fred frowned as he spoke. He was obviously thinking the same thing as the inspector—that this Oscar was something out of the ordinary. Ten to one he lived in the district, but he didn't share in its life. One couldn't place him, or imagine what his existence must be. To all appearances he played a lone hand—that was what chiefly struck them both.

'Do you think he'll try to get rid of Philippe?'

'We shall know before morning.'

'I went into the tobacconist's in the Rue de Douai just now. They're old pals of mine. I don't think anyone knows the district better than they do. They get every possible type of customer, according to the time of day. And yet they're completely fogged, too.'

'All the same, Arlette must have been meeting him somewhere.'

'At his own home, perhaps?'

Maigret would have sworn that wasn't it.

Which was possibly rather absurd. Because practically nothing was known about him, Oscar was taking on terrifying proportions. In the long run one began to be influenced in spite of oneself, by the mystery that surrounded him, and perhaps to credit him with more brains than he really had.

He was like a shadow—always more impressive than the solid object that casts it.

After all he was only a man, a flesh-and-blood man, who'd worked as valet and chauffeur and always been keen on women.

The last time he'd been seen in his true light had been at Nice. He was probably responsible for the pregnancy of little Antoinette Méjat, who'd died of it; Maria Pinaco had been his mistress too, and now she was a prostitute.

Then, a few years later, he'd bought a house near the place where he was born—typical of a self-made man who'd suddenly got hold of money. He went back to parade his new fortune in front of those who had seen him in his days of poverty.

'Is that you, sir?'

The telephone again, with the standard opening. Lapointe's job was to report progress.

'I'm speaking from a little bar in the Place Constantin-Pecqueur. He went into a house in the Rue Caulaincourt, and up to the fifth floor. He knocked on a door there, but nobody answered.'

'What does the concierge say?'

'That a painter lives there, a Bohemian type.

173

She doesn't know whether he takes drugs, but says he often looks strange. She's seen Philippe go up there before. Sometimes he's spent the night there.'

'Is the painter a homo?'

'Probably. She doesn't believe there are such people; but she's never seen him with a woman.'

'What's Philippe doing now?'

'He's turned to the right, towards the Sacré-Cœur.'

'Nobody seems to be following him?'

'Nobody except us. Everything's O.K. It's begun to rain and it's damn' cold. If I'd known, I'd have put on a sweater.'

Madame Rose had covered the table with a red-checked cloth, and placed a steaming soup-tureen in the middle. Four places were laid: Arlette's successor, who had got back into a navy-blue suit in which she looked like a well brought-up young girl, was helping to serve, and it was hard to realize that only a few minutes earlier she had been standing naked in the middle of the dance-floor.

'I'd be surprised if he never came here,' said Maigret.

'To see her?'

'Well, she was his pupil. I wonder if he was jealous.'

That was a question to which Fred would certainly know the answer; for Fred, too, had had women who went to bed with other men—he even forced them to do so—and must know how a man felt in such circumstances.

'He'd never be jealous of the men she met here,' he said.

'Are you sure?'

'Well, he must have been so self-confident. He was convinced he'd got a firm hold and that she'd never escape.'

Was it the Countess who had pushed her old husband over the precipice, from the terrace of The Oasis? Most likely. If Oscar had done it, he wouldn't have had such a hold over her. Even if he'd been an accomplice.

There was a certain irony in the whole story. The poor Count had been crazy about his wife, putting up with all her whims and humbly begging her to keep a little corner for him in her shadow. If he had not loved her so much, she might have put up with him. It was the very intensity of his adoration that she had found intolerable.

Had Oscar foreseen that that would happen one day? Had he been spying on her? Very probably.

It was easy to imagine the scene. The couple had gone out on to the terrace when they got back from the Casino, and the Countess had had no difficulty in leading the old man to the edge of the precipice and then pushing him over.

When she turned round, she must have been terrified to see that the chauffeur had been watching, and was now staring silently at her.

What had passed between them? What agreement had they reached?

In any case, it was not the gigolos who had

squandered all her money—a good share of it must have gone to Oscar.

He was too shrewd to stay with her. He had disappeared, and waited for several years before buying that house near his birthplace.

He had done nothing to attract attention, he hadn't started throwing money about.

Maigret always found himself back at the same point: the man was a lone wolf, and he had learnt that lone wolves were not to be trusted.

Bonvoisin was known to have a taste for women—the old cook's description had been revealing. Before meeting Arlette at La Bourboule, he must have had other women.

Had he trained them in the same way? Kept as firm a hold over them? There had never been a scandal to call attention to him.

The Countess had begun to go downhill, and nobody spoke of him. She used to give him money. He must live not far off, somewhere in the district; yet a man like Fred, who had been employing Arlette for two years, had never been able to find out anything about him.

And now, perhaps, it was his turn to be trapped as the Count had been. Wasn't it quite likely that Arlette had been trying to get rid of him? In fact she *had* tried at least once—after that impassioned discussion with Lapointe.

'What I can't understand,' said Fred—as though Maigret had been uttering his thoughts aloud, while he ate his soup—'is why he killed that crazy old woman. He's supposed to have been after the jewels she kept hidden in her mattress. It's possible he was—in fact it's certain. But he had a hold over her, and he could have got them some other way.'

'There's no saying she'd have let them go so easily,' objected Rose. 'They were all she had left, and she must have been trying to make them last. Besides, remember, she doped, and those people are apt to talk too much.'

Arlette's successor understood not a word of this, and sat staring curiously at each of them in turn. Fred had found her in a little theatre where she had a walking-on part. She was very proud of being promoted to a solo act, but one could feel she was rather afraid of meeting the same fate as Arlette.

'Will you be staying on this evening?' she asked Maigret.

'Perhaps. I don't know.'

'The inspector may leave in two minutes' time, or he may stay till tomorrow morning,' said Fred with a sly smile.

'If you ask me,' remarked Rose, 'Arlette was fed up with him, and he knew it. A man can hold a woman like that for a time, especially when she's very young. But she'd met other men. . . .'

She stared rather hard at her husband.

'Hadn't she, Fred? They'd made offers to her. And it isn't only women who can feel that kind of thing coming. I wouldn't be surprised if he'd decided to get hold of a lot of money at one stroke, and take her away to live somewhere else. Only he made the mistake of being too sure of himself, and told her about his plans. He's not the first to have been ruined that way.'

All this was still rather confused, of course; but the truth was beginning to take shape, in a way which shed a clearer light on the sinister figure of Oscar.

Again the telephone rang, but when Maigret went he found the call was not for him, but for Fred—who took the receiver, and courteously refrained from shutting the cloakroom door.

'Hello?' they heard him say, 'Yes . . . What? . . . What are you doing there? Yes. . . . Yes, he's here. . . . Don't shout so loud, you're deafening me. . . . O.K. . . . Yes, I know. . . . Why? . . . But that's idiotic. . . . You'd better speak to him yourself. . . . All right. I don't know what he'll decide to do. . . . Stay where you are. . . . Probably he'll come along and join you. . . .'

He came back to the table looking rather worried.

'That was the Grasshopper,' he murmured, as though to himself.

He sat down, but did not go on with his meal at once.

'I wonder what's at the back of his mind. He's been working for me for five years, but I never know what he's thinking. He's never even told me where he lives. For all I can tell, he may have a wife and family.'

'Where is he now?' inquired Maigret.

'Up at the top of the *Butte*, at Chez Francis,

the little restaurant at the corner, where there's always a bearded fellow telling fortunes. You know where I mean?'

Fred pondered, searching for an explanation.

'The funny thing is that Inspector Lognon is walking up and down just opposite.'

'What's the Grasshopper doing up there?'

'He didn't tell me exactly. I gathered it was something to do with that chap Philippe. The Grasshopper knows every pansy in Montmartre —in fact I used to wonder if he wasn't one himself. And between ourselves, it's possible he does a bit of drug-peddling at odd moments. I know you won't take advantage of that, and I promise you there's never any brought in here.'

'Is Chez Francis one of Philippe's hang-outs?'

'So it would seem. The Grasshopper may know more about that.'

'That doesn't explain why he went there.'

'Very well—I'll tell you, if you haven't already guessed! But please understand that it's his own idea. He thinks we might just as well tip you the wink, because you'll bear it in mind and give us the benefit of the doubt if we should ever need it. In this line of business we have to keep on the right side of the police. Anyhow, he's probably not the only one who's on to this idea, since Lognon is already prowling around there.'

Seeing that Maigret did not move, Fred exclaimed in astonishment:

'Aren't you going up there?' Then he added:

'Oh, of course—you can't leave here, in case your inspectors ring up.'

All the same, Maigret went to the telephone.

'Torrence? Have you any men to spare? Three? Good! Send them up to the Place du Tertre and tell them to keep an eye on Chez Francis, the *bistrot* at the corner. Ring the district police too, and tell them to send some of their men up that way. No, I don't know exactly. I'm staying here.'

He was rather sorry, now, to have made Picratt's his headquarters, but didn't quite feel he ought to go up to the *Butte*.

The telephone rang. It was Lapointe again.

'I don't know what he's playing at, sir. For the last half-hour he's been weaving to and fro around Montmartre. I wonder if he suspects he's being followed, and is trying to shake us off. He went into a café in the Rue Lepic, and then down again to the Place Blanche, where he took a turn round the same two restaurants. Then he turned back up the Rue Lepic and branched into the Rue Tholozé, where he went into a house where there's a studio at the far end of the courtyard. An old woman lives there who used to be a *café-concert* singer.'

'Does she take drugs?'

'Yes. Jacquin went in to question her as soon as Philippe left. She's a kind of scruffier version of the Countess. She was tight. She started laughing, and swore she hadn't been able to give him what he wanted. "I haven't even got any for myself!" she said.'

'Where is he now?'

'Eating hard-boiled eggs in a bar in the Rue

Tholozé. It's raining cats and dogs. Everything's all right.'

'He'll probably go up to the Place du Tertre.'

'We nearly got that far just now, but he suddenly turned back. I wish he'd make up his mind. My feet are frozen.'

Rose and the new girl were clearing the table. Fred had fetched the brandy and was pouring some into the two balloon-glasses, while waiting for coffee.

'I shall soon have to go up and change,' he announced. 'That's not a hint for you to leave. Stay as long as you like. Here's how!'

'Do you suppose the Grasshopper knows Oscar?'

'Funny! That's just what I was thinking.'

'He goes to the races every afternoon, doesn't he?'

'Yes—and you mean the chances are that a man like Oscar, with nothing to do, will spend part of his time there too?'

He drained his glass, wiped his mouth, looked at the girl, who was wondering what to do next, and winked at Maigret.

'I'm going upstairs to change,' he announced. 'Come up for a minute, kid, I want to talk to you about your act.'

He winked at Maigret again, and added in an undertone:

'Helps to pass the time, you know!'

Maigret was left alone in the cabaret.

9

'He went up to the Place du Tertre, sir, and nearly ran into Inspector Lognon, who just had time to jump back into the shadow.'

'You're sure he didn't see him?'

'Quite sure. He went and looked in at the window of Chez Francis. In this weather there's hardly anyone there. A few regular customers, sitting gloomily over their drinks. He didn't go in. Then he turned into the Rue du Mont-Cenis and went down the steps to the Place Constantin-Pecqueur, where he stopped outside another café. There's a big stove in the middle of the floor, sawdust sprinkled around, marble-topped tables, and the *patron* is playing cards with some friends.'

The new girl at Picratt's came downstairs again, looking slightly embarrassed, and not knowing what to do with herself, came and sat beside Maigret. Perhaps so as not to leave him all alone. She had already put on the black silk dress that had belonged to Arlette.

'What's your name?'

'Geneviève. They're going to call me Dolly. I'm to be photographed tomorrow in this dress.'

'How old are you?'

'Twenty-three. Did you ever see Arlette do her act? Is it true she was so awfully good? I'm a bit awkward, aren't I?'

Next time Lapointe rang up, he sounded depressed.

'He's going round and round like a circus horse. We're following, and it's still raining cats and dogs. We've been back through the Place Clichy, and then to the Place Blanche, where he went round the same two restaurants again. As he's got no morphia, he's beginning to take a drink here and there. He hasn't found what he wants, and he's walking more slowly now, keeping in the shadow of the houses.'

'He still has no suspicions?'

'No. Janvier's had a chat with Inspector Lognon. Lognon went back to all the places Philippe visited last night, and that's how he came to hear of Chez Francis. He was just told that Philippe went there now and again, and that probably someone supplied him with dope.'

'Is the Grasshopper still there?'

'No, he left a few minutes ago. At the moment, Philippe is on his way down the steps in the Rue du Mont-Cenis again, most likely to have another look in the café in the Place Constantin-Pecqueur.'

Tania and the Grasshopper came in together. It was still too early to turn on Picratt's neon sign, but evidently they were all in the habit of arriving in good time. Everybody seemed pretty much at home. Rose put her head round the door before going upstairs to change. She was still holding a dishcloth.

'Oh, there you are!' she said to the new girl.

Then, looking her up and down, she added:

'Another evening, don't put your dress on so soon. It wears it out unnecessarily.'

And to Maigret she said, in conclusion:

'Help yourself, Inspector. That's what the bottle's for.'

Tania seemed to be in a bad temper. She stared at Arlette's successor and gave a slight shrug.

'Move up a bit, I want to sit down,' she told the girl.

She stared hard at Maigret, and then inquired:

'You haven't caught him yet?'

'I expect to catch him tonight.'

'You don't think it's occurred to him to cut and run?'

She knew something, too. In fact everybody had some scrap of knowledge. He'd had the same impression the night before. And now Tania was wondering whether she wouldn't be wise to tell what she knew.

'Did you ever meet him with Arlette?'

'I don't even know who he is or what he looks like.'

'But you know he exists?'

'I've a shrewd suspicion.'

'What else do you know?'

'Where he hangs out, perhaps.'

Helpfulness was not her habit, and she spoke sulkily, as though it went against the grain.

'My dressmaker lives in the Rue Caulaincourt, just opposite the Place Constantin-Pecqueur. I'm asleep most of the day, so I usually go there about five o'clock in the afternoon. Twice, I've seen Arlette get off a bus at the corner of the *place* and walk across it.'

'In what direction?'

'Towards the steps.'

'It didn't occur to you to follow her?'

'Why should I have followed her?'

That was a lie. She was inquisitive. By the time she got to the foot of the steps, Arlette had presumably vanished.

'Is that all you know?'

'That's all. He must live somewhere there.'

Maigret had poured himself a glass of brandy, and was in no hurry to get up when the telephone rang again.

'He's still at the same game, sir.'

'Hanging round the café in the Place Constantin-Pecqueur?'

'Yes. The only places where he stops now are there, at the two restaurants in the Place Blanche, and outside Chez Francis.'

'Is Lognon still up there?'

'Yes. I just caught a glimpse of him as I went past.'

'Ask him from me to go down to the Place Constantin-Pecqueur and have a word with the proprietor. Not in front of the customers, if he can avoid it. Tell him to ask whether he knows Oscar Bonvoisin—and if not, to give a description of him, because he may be known there by some other name.'

'Right away?'

'Yes. He'll have the time, while Philippe's on his round. Tell him to ring me up as soon as he's done it.'

When he went back into the cabaret, the Grasshopper was there, pouring himself a drink at the bar.

'Not caught him yet?'

'How did you get the tip about Chez Francis?'

'From some pansies. They all know one another, in that bunch. First they told me about a bar in the Rue Caulaincourt where Philippe goes from time to time, and then about Chez Francis, where he sometimes looks in late at night.'

'Do they know Oscar?'

'Yes.'

'Bonvoisin?'

'They don't know his surname. They told me he's a local man who comes in now and again for a glass of white wine before bedtime.'

'Does he know Philippe?'

'Everyone's on speaking terms in that place;

186

he behaves like the rest of them. You can't say I haven't helped you.'

'Has he been seen today?'

'No. Nor yesterday.'

'Did they tell you where he lives?'

'Somewhere in the neighbourhood.'

Time was dragging now, and one began to feel as though nothing would ever happen. Jean-Jean, the accordionist, came in and went to the cloakroom to wipe his muddy shoes and comb his hair.

'Not got Arlette's murderer yet?' he inquired.

Then came another telephone call from Lapointe.

'I passed on your instructions to Inspector Lognon. He's gone to the Place Constantin-Pecqueur. Philippe's just gone into Chez Francis and is having a drink, but there's no one there who answers to the description of Oscar. Lognon will ring you. I told him where you were. Was that right?'

Lapointe's voice didn't sound the same as at the beginning of the evening. Every time he wanted to telephone, he had to go into some bar or other. This was his umpteenth phone call; and no doubt he had a drop of something on each occasion, to warm himself.

Fred came downstairs, resplendent in his dinner-jacket, with an imitation diamond in his starched shirt-front, and his freshly-shaven face a pleasant shade of pink.

'Get along up and change now,' he said to Tania.

Then he went to turn on the lights and straighten the rows of bottles behind the bar.

The second musician, Monsieur Dupeu, had just arrived in his turn when Lognon at last rang up.

'Where are you speaking from?' inquired Maigret.

'From Chez Manière, in the Rue Caulaincourt. I've been to the Place Constantin-Pecqueur and I've got the address!'

He was in a state of great excitement.

'Did they give it to you without any fuss?'

'The *patron* didn't suspect anything. I didn't tell him I was a policeman. I pretended I was up from the country, and looking for a friend.'

'Do they call him by name?'

'They call him Monsieur Oscar.'

'Where does he live?'

'Above the steps, on the right, in a little house with a plot of garden in front. There's a wall all round—the house can't be seen from the street.'

'He's not been to the Place Constantin-Pecqueur today?'

'No. They waited for him to begin their game, for he's usually punctual. That was why the proprietor was playing, instead of him.'

'What has he told them he does in life?'

'Nothing. He doesn't talk much. They think he has private means—seems comfortably off. He's a very good *belote* player. He often drops in during the morning, about eleven, for a glass of white wine before doing his shopping.'

188

'He does his own shopping? Hasn't he got a servant?'

'No. And no charwoman. They think he's a bit eccentric.'

'Wait for me somewhere near the steps.'

Maigret finished his brandy and went to the cloakroom to fetch his heavy overcoat, which was still damp; the two musicians began to play a few notes, as though to warm themselves up.

'In the bag?' inquired Fred from behind the bar.

'Soon will be, perhaps.'

'Come back here, won't you? We'll have a bottle of champagne on it.'

The Grasshopper called a taxi. As he was shutting the door, he said below his breath:

'If it's the chap I've heard some vague talk about, you'd best take care. He's a tough customer.'

Water was streaming down the windows of the taxi, and the lights of the town could be seen only through a close-striped curtain of rain. Philippe must be splashing through that, somewhere, with the inspectors following him in the shadows.

Maigret got out and walked across the Place Constantin-Pecqueur, where he found Lognon flattened against a wall.

'I've identified the house.'

'Any light showing?'

'I looked over the wall. Nothing to be seen. I suppose the pansy doesn't know the address. What do we do now?'

189

'Is there any way out at the back?'

'No. This is the only door.'

'We're going in. You've got a gun?'

Lognon merely pointed to his pocket. There was a dilapidated wall, like that of a country garden, overhung by branches of trees. Lognon set to work on the lock, and it took him several minutes, while the inspector stood on guard.

Once the door opened, they found themselves looking across a small garden towards one of those small, low houses of which a few are still hidden in the byways of Montmartre. It was in complete darkness.

'Go and get the front door open, and then come back here,' said Maigret—who, despite skilled tuition, was a poor hand at picking a lock.

'Wait for me outside the gate, and when the others come past, tell Lapointe or Janvier I'm here, and that they're to keep on trailing Philippe.'

Inside the house there was not a sound, not a sign of life. But Maigret kept his revolver in his hand. The passage was warm and had a countrified smell: Bonvoisin must use wood for heating. It was a damp house. He hesitated for a moment and then, with a shrug, turned the electric switch he had just found on his right.

To his surprise, the place was very clean; it did not have the dejected and rather grubby appearance of most bachelors' homes. The passage was lit by a lantern with coloured glass panes. Maigret opened the right-hand door and found himself in a drawing-room of the type to be seen

190

in the windows of furniture emporiums—in deplorable taste, but prosperous-looking, with everything made of the heaviest available wood. Next came a dining-room, furnished from the same source in an imitation Provençal style, with plastic fruit on a silver dish.

There was not a speck of dust to be seen, and he found the same spotless cleanliness in the kitchen. The fire was not yet out in the stove, and there was warm water in the kettle. Opening cupboards, he saw bread, meat, butter and eggs, and there was a bin containing carrots, turnips and a cauliflower. The house evidently had no cellar, for there was a cask of wine, too, with a glass turned upside-down on the bung, as though it were in frequent use.

There was one more room on the ground floor —across the corridor, opposite the drawing-room. It was a biggish bedroom, with silk-shaded lamps that gave a very feminine touch, and a satin eiderdown on the bed. It had a profusion of mirrors too, reminding Maigret of certain brothels, and there were almost as many in the bathroom next door.

Except for the food in the kitchen, the cask of wine, and the embers in the stove, there was not a sign of life. Nothing was out of place, as happens even in the best-run house. There were no ashes in the ash-trays. No dirty linen or shabby clothes in the cupboards.

He understood why, when he went upstairs and opened the two landing doors—not without apprehension, for the silence, broken only by the rain drumming on the roof, was rather nerve-racking.

There was nobody there.

The room on the left was Oscar Bonvoisin's real bedroom, where he spent his solitary nights. Here the bed was an iron one, covered with thick red blankets; it had not been made, and the sheets were none too clean; on the bedside table lay some fruit, including an apple which had been bitten into, its flesh already brown.

There was a pair of muddy shoes on the floor, two or three packets of cigarettes, and a liberal scattering of cigarette-ends.

Though there was a proper bathroom downstairs, this upper floor had nothing but a hand-basin in the corner of the bedroom, with one tap, and a few dirty towels lying around. A pair of trousers hung from a hook.

Maigret sought in vain for papers. The drawers yielded a mixed harvest, including cartridges for an automatic pistol, but not a single letter or document.

Going downstairs again, however, he found a drawer full of photographs in the bedroom chest of drawers. The films were there too, together with the camera and a flash-lamp.

Not all the photos were of Arlette. At least twenty women, all young and shapely, had posed for Bonvoisin in the same erotic attitudes. Some of the photographs had been enlarged. Looking for the dark-room, Maigret found it upstairs; there was a red electric lamp hanging above a sink, and a great many little bottles of chemicals.

He was on his way down when he heard steps outside, and flattened himself against the wall, pointing his revolver at the door.

'It's me, sir,' said a voice.

Janvier stood there, water streaming off him, his hat soaked out of all shape.

'Have you found anything?' he asked.

'What's Philippe doing?'

'Still going round in circles. I don't know how he manages to stand up by now. He had a squabble with a flower-seller opposite the Moulin Rouge—he'd asked her for dope. She told me about it afterwards. She knows him by sight. He implored her to tell him where he could find some. Then he went into a telephone-box and rang up Dr. Bloch, saying that he was at the end of his tether, and making all kinds of threats. If it goes on much longer he'll throw a fit in the middle of the street.'

Janvier looked round at the empty house, where lights were burning in every room.

'You don't suppose the bird has flown?'

His breath smelt of alcohol, and his lips were twisted in a slight, tense smile that Maigret knew well.

'Aren't you having the railway people warned?'

'Judging by the fire in the stove, he left the house at least three or four hours ago. In other words, if he means to run away he'll have got on a train long ago. He had plenty to choose from.'

'Still, we could warn the frontier stations.'

Strangely enough, Maigret felt not the slightest inclination to set the cumbersome police mechanism in motion. True, it was only a hunch; but he felt certain the affair was going to be settled in Montmartre, where everything had happened so far.

'You think he's watching for Philippe somewhere?' asked Janvier.

The inspector shrugged his shoulders. He had no idea. He went outside and found Lognon, flat against the garden wall.

'You'd better put out the lights and stay here to keep watch,' he said.

'Do you think he'll come back?'

He thought nothing at all.

'I say, Lognon, what were the addresses where Philippe went last night?'

The inspector had made a note of them all. Since his release, the young man had been back to every one of them, in vain.

'You're sure you haven't left any out?'

Lognon was offended.

'I've told you all I know. There's only one other address and that's his own, in the Boulevard Rochechouart.'

Maigret said nothing, but he lit his pipe with an air of quiet satisfaction.

'Good. Stay here, just in case. Janvier, you come with me.'

'Have you had an idea?'

'I think I know where we shall find him.'

They walked, with coat-collars turned up and hands thrust deep in their pockets. It wasn't worth taking a taxi.

As they reached the Place Blanche they caught sight of Philippe in the distance, coming out of one of the two restaurants. A little way behind him was young Lapointe, still wearing his cap; he made them a slight sign.

The others were not far off, still keeping watch on Philippe.

'You come with us,' said Maigret to Lapointe.

They had only five hundred yards still to go, along the almost deserted Boulevard. The night-clubs, whose neon lights were gleaming through the rain, couldn't be doing much business in weather like this, and the doorkeepers in their gold-braided uniforms were keeping under shelter, ready to open their big red umbrellas.

'Where are we going?' asked Lapointe.

'To Philippe's house.'

For the Countess had been killed in her own flat. And the murderer had been waiting for Arlette at her home in the Rue Notre-Dame de Lorette.

It was an old building. Above the shuttered ground-floor windows was a book-binder's sign, and, to the right of the entrance, that of a book-seller. They were obliged to ring for the *cordon* to be pulled. The door opened silently, the three men stepped into a dimly-lit corridor, and Maigret signed to the others to make as little noise as possible. As they went past the concierge's door he growled out an indistinguishable name, and then they began to climb the uncarpeted stairs.

On the first floor one of the door-mats was

wet, and a ray of light could be seen under the door. From there until they reached the sixth floor, they were in pitch darkness, for the *minuterie* had gone out.

'Let me go first, sir,' whispered Lapointe, trying to slip past between Maigret and the wall.

The inspector pushed him back with a firm hand. He knew from Lognon that Philippe's attic was the third room on the left on this top floor. His electric torch showed him that the narrow corridor, with its yellowing walls, was empty; he pressed the button of the *minuterie* and the light came on again.

He placed one of his men to either side of the third door, and took hold of the door handle, his revolver ready in the other hand. The handle turned. The door was not locked.

He pushed it with his toe and then stood motionless, listening. As in the house he had just left, he could hear nothing but the rain beating on the roof and water flowing through the drainpipes. It seemed to him that he could hear his companions' hearts beating as well; his own too, perhaps.

He put out his hand and found the electric light switch, just inside the door.

There was nobody in the room. There was no cupboard to hide in. Bonvoisin's room—the upstairs one—had been luxurious compared to this. There were no sheets on the bed. There was a chamber-pot that had not been emptied. There were dirty clothes on the floor.

Lapointe bent down and looked under the bed. No use. Not a soul in the place. The room stank.

Suddenly, Maigret had the impression of a movement behind him. To the stupefaction of the two inspectors, he bounded backwards, gave a half-turn, and heaved vigorously with his shoulder against the opposite door.

The door yielded. It was not shut. There was someone behind it, someone who had been watching them, and it was the faintest movement of the door which had caught Maigret's attention.

He had thrust so hard across the passage that he was flung forward into the room, and was saved from falling only because he collided with a man almost as heavy as himself.

The room was in darkness, and it was Janvier who had the sense to turn on the light.

'Look out, sir. . . .'

Maigret had already been butted in the chest. He reeled, but saved himself from falling by clutching at something that pitched over with a crash—a bedside table with some china object on it.

He grabbed his revolver by the barrel and tried to strike a blow with the butt. He didn't know the elusive Oscar, but he had recognized him— this was the man described to him, the man he had been seeing all this time in his imagination. The fellow had bent double again and was charging at the two inspectors who were barring his way.

Lapointe clutched automatically at his jacket, while Janvier tried to get a grip on his body.

They had no time to look at one another. There was a body lying on the bed, but they could pay no attention to that.

Janvier was knocked down, Lapointe was left with the jacket in his hands, and a figure was darting down the corridor, when a shot rang out. For a moment they didn't realize who had fired. It was Lapointe, who was too frightened to look in the direction of the fugitive, and was staring at his revolver with a kind of bewildered astonishment.

Bonvoisin staggered on for a few paces, bending forward, and finally collapsed on the floor.

'Take care, Janvier. . . .'

He had an automatic pistol in his hand. The barrel was moving. Then, slowly, the fingers opened and the weapon fell to the ground.

'D'you think I've killed him, sir?'

Lapointe's eyes were starting from his head, and his lips quivering. He couldn't believe it was he who had done such a thing, and he looked again at his revolver, in respectful astonishment.

'I've killed him!' he repeated, still not daring to look at the body.

Janvier was bending over it.

'He's dead. You got him full in the chest.'

Maigret thought for a moment that Lapointe was going to faint. He laid a hand on his shoulder.

'Your first, is he?' he asked gently.

Then, to cheer the lad up, he added:

'Don't forget he killed Arlette.'

'So he did. . . .'

It was amusing to see the childish expression on Lapointe's face; he didn't know whether to laugh or cry.

Cautious steps were heard on the stairs. A voice asked:

'Has anyone been hurt?'

'Don't let them come up,' said Maigret to Janvier.

He turned to attend to the human figure he had seen for a second on the bed. It was a girl of sixteen or seventeen—the bookseller's servant. She was not dead, but a towel had been tied over her face to keep her from shouting. Her hands were tied behind her back and her slip was pushed right up to her armpits.

'Go down and ring up headquarters,' said Maigret to Lapointe. 'If you can find a *bistrot* that's still open, have a drink while you're about it.'

'Oh—do you think . . . ?'

'It's an order.'

It was some little time before the girl could speak. She had come up to her room about half past ten, after a visit to the cinema. Before she had even had time to turn on the light, she had been seized by an unknown man who had been waiting for her in the dark, and he had tied the towel tightly over her mouth. Then he had bound her hands and thrown her on the bed.

After that he had paid no attention to her for a time. He was listening to the sounds in the house; and every now and then he opened the door a crack. He was waiting for Philippe, but he was suspicious, and that was why he did not wait in the young man's own room. He had no doubt inspected it before crossing to the maid's attic, and that explained why the door had been open.

'What happened after that?'

'He took my clothes off—and he had to tear them, because of my hands being tied.'

'Did he rape you?'

She nodded, and began to cry. Then, picking up a heap of light-coloured material from the floor, she said:

'My dress is ruined. . . .'

She didn't realize what a narrow escape she had had. It was most unlikely that Bonvoisin would have left her behind him, alive. She had seen him, just as Philippe had seen him. If he had not strangled her at once, like the other two, it was no doubt because he planned to have a little more fun with her while waiting for the young man to arrive.

*

By three o'clock in the morning, Oscar Bonvoisin's body was lying in one of the metal drawers at the mortuary, not far from those of Arlette and the Countess.

Philippe, after a row with a customer at Chez Francis, where he had finally gone in, had been taken to the local police station by a uniformed policeman. Torrence had gone to bed. The inspectors who had been going the round from the Place Blanche to the Place du Tertre and from there to the Place Constantin-Pecqueur, had gone home too.

Leaving police headquarters on the Quai des Orfèvres with Lapointe and Janvier, Maigret had suggested, after a moment's hesitation:

'What about a bottle of champagne?'

'Where?'

'At Picratt's.'

'Not for me,' said Janvier. 'My wife will be waiting for me, and the baby wakes us early.'

Lapointe said nothing. But he followed Maigret into the taxi.

They reached the Rue Pigalle just in time to see the new girl do her act. Fred came to meet them as they went in.

'In the bag?' he inquired.

Maigret nodded; and a few moments later a bucket with a bottle of champagne appeared on their table—which, as it so happened, was number six. The black dress was slipping slowly down over the white body of the girl, who was gazing at them with a scared expression, she was reluctant to uncover her belly and as soon as her nakedness was revealed she put both hands to cover it, as she had done at the evening rehearsal.

Did Fred do it on purpose? At that precise moment he should have turned off the spotlight and left the room in darkness, giving the dancer time to pick up her dress and hold it in front of her. But the spotlight did not go out, and the poor girl, completely at a loss, decided, after a long pause, to scuttle off to the kitchen—thus displaying a round, white behind.

The few clients in the place burst out laughing. Maigret thought Lapointe was laughing too; but looking more closely, he saw that tears were running down the inspector's cheeks.

'I beg your pardon,' he stammered. 'I ought not to. . . . I know it's stupid. But you see I . . . I loved her!'

He was even more ashamed when he woke up next morning, for he had no notion whatever of how he had got home.

His sister, who seemed to be in a particularly cheerful mood—Maigret had had a word with her—greeted him, as she drew back the curtains, with:

'A fine idea, having yourself put to bed by the inspector!'

That night, Lapointe had buried his first love. And killed his first man. As for Lognon, nobody had thought to release him from his watch, and he was still shivering on the steps above the Place Constantin-Pecqueur.